AGAINST THE BLACK

By Lilli Lindbeck

AGAINST THE BLACK

Copyright © 2019 by Lilli Lindbeck.

This book is based on a true story. Real life events establish the basis of the structure of this book, but the exact situations, the dialogue and some relationships have been fictionalized. The names of the original people have been changed, characters added, situations altered, and the characters have their own personalities and choices that are not those of the real people. While the names of authors, artists, organizations and some businesses are real, the majority of names, characters, events and incidents either are the product of the author's imagination or are used fictitiously; for that reason, any resemblance to actual persons, living or dead is entirely coincidental.

Book and Cover Design by Jason Buch

ISBN: 9781795232739

First Edition: January 2019

10 9 8 7 6 5 4 3 2 1

How to read this book

The main character of this book surrounds herself with music and frequently has music playing in her head. For this reason, a *theme song* has been chosen by the author to set the tone for each chapter. While most of the theme songs are dated prior to or during the time frame of the story (1994-1997), some of the songs are more recent. By contrast, all of the songs playing in the main character's head are appropriate to the time frame of the story.

The author has no rights to any of the songs referenced, but encourages the reader to support the artists by purchasing the songs and listening to them—either while reading the book or after reading it. Hopefully, some of the songs will be new to the reader. Some versions of the songs referenced are performed by an artist who did not write the song but whose performance of the song would have been preferred by the main character.

CHAPTER ONE

"Here I Go Again" - Whitesnake

"I understand I'm interrupting your plans for the evening." Maddy turned to see where the gentle, deep voice was coming from—and looking up, she had to catch her breath as she saw a man about 6-foot tall, wearing a black turtle neck and black pants, with close-cut black hair whose eyes pierced hers. He spoke with an eastern European accent and smiled wryly. She suddenly found herself speechless, and managed only to stutter, "Um, well, uh, I guess it's okay—no, it's fine."

Maddy was standing outside Fat Tuesdays with her friend Karen, whom she had recruited to go with her to lend moral support while she gathered her things from the condo of a man she had dated during the summer. She had met him in the spring while volunteering with an AIDS service organization and had been impressed with his professionalism. But by the end of the summer, she realized that he had two very different lives: one outside a bottle and the other lost inside one. Karen was tossing the last bag into the car when she said, "Why don't we go to Fat Tuesdays?" Maddy sighed, "Okay, I guess I can just have a Diet Coke." Maddy didn't drink hard liquor any more—and Fat Tuesdays specialized in daiquiris. "I'll go—just promise me this: <u>no men</u>! I'm swearing off men for a while! And I have my Friday morning wrap-up meeting at work tomorrow, so it can't be too late, okay?"

They had not been at Fat Tuesdays long, when two men approached them and asked Karen for a light from her cigarette. Karen readily struck up a conversation with them. Maddy purposefully ignored them but noticed that they had thick eastern European accents that she didn't hear often in Atlanta. A bit later, Karen whispered, "They want to take us dancing—let's go!" But Maddy practically shouted, "What? You swore: <u>no men</u>! This was supposed to be a girls-only night—I am seriously NOT in the mood for this." "Please, come on—it'll be fun!" Karen begged, "I helped you out, right?" Maddy sighed, "Okay, fine, but not too late—I told you I have that meeting tomorrow morning." One of the men said, "We have another guy with us—we'll get him and meet you out front." "Oh, great, now there are three of them!" Maddy was now scowling at Karen, furious.

"My name is Miklos Takács. I am in Atlanta painting a mural for a restaurant—we are just here from New York. What is your name?" Maddy struggled to find her voice, "Uh, my name is Maddy... Maddy Rose Anderson." When they got to the club, Miklos slipped in front of Maddy in line and paid for both of them, then immediately grabbed her hand and took her into the middle of the dance floor. Miklos was an amazing dancer, and when Maddy got too tired and wanted to stop, he simply lifted her up and danced with her legs around his waist! Before she knew it, he was helicoptering her in a circle, and everyone was watching! Finally leaving the dance floor, Miklos said, "Can I get you something to drink?" Maddy said, "I'm sorry, but I really have to go—I have to be at work early tomorrow." Miklos said, "In that case, I'll walk you to your car." Karen had decided to stay at the club, so Maddy walked out with Miklos, who said, "I am in town just a couple more days on this job—maybe I could call you?" Maddy wrote her home number down on her business card, and Miklos kissed her goodnight. She drove back to her home in Smyrna in a trance.

She had asked Miklos to call her at the house rather than at work, but Maddy still jumped all day, every time the phone in her office rang. Karen called to say she took one of the guys home and dropped him off at the restaurant this morning on her way to work—it was okay but nothing special. Maddy couldn't judge; she'd been in Karen's shoes for most of the 80's, but was determined that the '90's would be different. The year before, she had started working with a Jungian therapist who was helping her to examine her low self-esteem (rooted in childhood issues), to set healthier boundaries and to treat herself better. As part of that work, she had stopped drinking hard liquor and adopted a "30-day rule", which meant she didn't sleep with a guy until they had dated for 30 days. At least it was a way of protecting herself from one-night stands. Plus, her volunteer work in the AIDS community had taught her that one-night stands could be deadly.

When she got home, she checked her answering machine, but the only message was from the lawn guy who said he couldn't make it this Saturday and would check back next week. She put a couple Van Halen CDs into the player and went upstairs to change and finish sewing her African dance outfit for class on Saturday. Back in April, Maddy had flown to New Orleans to see JazzFest and had been mesmerized by the African dancers—it reminded her of seeing Zulu dancers when she was in South Africa a few years earlier. But just as she was laying out the fabric pieces on the table, the phone rang. She could barely hear him through the receiver because her heart was pounding so loudly. Miklos said, "Thank you so much for going to the club with us—I had such a wonderful time dancing with you." Maddy stammered, "Oh, yes, uh, me too." Miklos continued, "The murals are almost done—we should be finished by the end of the day tomorrow—could I see you tomorrow night? I'm afraid I don't have a car here." Maddy said, "Oh, sure, no problem—I can pick you up at the restaurant—maybe we can just come back here, have dinner, listen to music and hang out—then I can take you back to where you are staying." After getting the name and address of the restaurant to get directions from Smyrna, Maddy finally allowed herself to believe it and burst into a grin—he called!

Saturday morning at African dance class, Maddy could not keep her mind on the "Funga Alafia" that was being taught. Her mind was spinning—what to wear, what music to put on and what to make for dinner …. Miklos was ready when she arrived at the restaurant and explained that he had been painting murals for restaurants in New York—this was a chain, so they wanted the same murals for the restaurant they were opening in Atlanta. He explained that the two guys he with him on Thursday night at Fat Tuesdays primarily handle the prep work for the walls, then Miklos painted the mural once the walls were ready. Miklos asked Maddy what she did, "I'm a management consultant for a national company, so I travel to meet with clients and to do speaking engagements." "Do you have any clients in New York?" he asked. "No—they are mostly in the southeast and Midwest." She had a mix tape playing in the car, and Miklos said, "In New York, I hear music constantly—in the subways, on the streets—and all kinds of music. Have you ever heard of a didgeridoo?" Maddy said, "No, what's that?" He described a 3-foot long wooden tube that you blow through and said, "I have a tape from one of the guys in the subway who plays one—I'll send it to you when I get back. Have you been to New York before?" Maddy said, "No—have you lived there long?"

Miklos explained that he was born in Budapest, Hungary—of course it was Communist then—the last of the troops just left three years ago. He said he hated living under Communism—so he escaped in 1980, finding people to help him get into Austria. He lived there for a few years, and then came to New York.

They grilled steaks outside and the evening flew by. After they finished the dishes, Miklos said, "It is such a beautiful evening, do you have a blanket or something we could spread out in the backyard—I would like to look at the stars—in the city, you can't see the stars." Maddy grabbed a blanket from the closet and spread it out—soon they were lying next to one another, and Miklos held her hand. Maddy thought, "This is the best evening that I can remember."

On the drive back to the hotel where Miklos was staying, he said, "Maddy, could I call you when I get back to New York? Maybe you could come visit or I could come back here?" Maddy said, "Absolutely." Driving back home to Smyrna, she replayed parts of the weekend in her head—it felt like a dream. Maddy always had music on wherever she was—even a local jazz radio station playing at the office all day while she worked—and usually woke up with a song playing in her head. Tonight, one of her favorite songs by the Bodeans, "Dreams" was playing in her head—dreams were definitely made of this.

CHAPTER TWO

"Split Decision" – Steve Winwood

For the next two months, Miklos and Maddy talked on the phone and mailed letters, postcards, and music tapes back and forth. Miklos called her *"Rózsa"*—it meant rose in Hungarian—he said her middle name suited her better, because she was like a rose to him. It was approaching Thanksgiving, so Maddy invited Miklos to spend it with her. She was nervous, because he would be staying overnight, and they had only kissed on his first trip to Atlanta. This trip would be just one night, because he was finishing up a painting job here and had another job booked back in New York on Saturday, so he had to fly in Thursday morning and out on Friday evening.

She had learned that in addition to doing murals, Miklos did faux finishing to make walls and other surfaces look like marble, stone or wood. Inspired, Maddy took a workshop on faux finishing and painted two short wooden pillars to look like green marble. She found a heavy piece of dark green glass with beveled edges at an industrial fabrication outlet and created a coffee table with it. When Miklos saw it, he teased her that she was going to move in on his territory. They laughed. She showed him the canvas floor mat in the kitchen that she had stenciled with flowers and ribbon; then showed him the three fabric panels in the living room that she had painted with three dancers and the words "Dance on Life." Then she brought out the quilt she sewed for her grandmother's 100th birthday (it was returned to Maddy after her grandmother died). She also showed him a scrapbook of the cakes she had decorated. Miklos said, "Rózsa, I had no idea you were so talented!" Maddy shook her head and said, "You have more natural ability in one of your little fingers than I have in my whole body! I am just curious and love learning new things. My grandmother said, 'Stay curious. Never stop learning new things—it will keep you young.' She lived to almost 101 and was sharp as a tack right up until the end! So I took her advice to heart."

Maddy had started the preparations for their Thanksgiving dinner the weekend before, including her favorite stuffing with dried fruit, candied fruit, and chestnuts. She baked an apple pie from scratch and a made a sweet potato casserole. Miklos said that for the ten years or so he'd lived in the U.S. most of the people he knew just ate out on Thanksgiving and didn't cook, so this was his first traditional homemade Thanksgiving. He was amazed that anyone would cook this much for a single meal!

After they finished doing the dishes and putting everything away, Miklos said, "Where would you like me to sleep?" Maddy closed her eyes and took a breath, "Well, we haven't actually had 'the talk' yet—I guess it's time for that." Miklos looked puzzled. Maddy explained, "I volunteer as an AIDS educator in Atlanta and have learned more than I ever wanted to about sexually transmitted diseases—I always tell people to talk honestly with the people they sleep with and use protection, so I've got to practice what I preach. I don't have anything that's sexually transmissible. Do you?"

A cloud came over Miklos's face; he sighed, looked down and after a while said, "I have herpes."

Maddy was genuinely taken aback. Of all the scenarios that she had played out in her mind, this was not one of them. She stammered, "Oh." Miklos said, "It happened before I came to America. She did not tell me she had it, and I got it. I do not want to treat you as she treated me, and I would not want you to have to suffer with this. I take medication, but I still get outbreaks sometimes."

There was a very loud argument going on inside Maddy's head, and she was having trouble focusing. She finally managed to stammer, "Uh, I actually don't know anything about herpes—I don't know anyone with it or what fluids the virus lives in—I'll have to read up on it and figure out how women protect themselves—if condoms are enough or what..." She suddenly realized that she had slipped into her educator persona and was embarrassed. "I'm sorry—I just—I wasn't prepared." Miklos gently said, "I understand." Maddy said, "Would you be okay if we slept in the same bed but didn't do anything?" He said, "Yes, of course."

By the next morning, Maddy was over the shock, and they were dancing in the living room to her Gipsy Kings CD. They heated up leftover apple pie in the microwave and put vanilla ice cream on it. When it was time to leave for the airport, Maddy took Miklos's hand and said, "Babe, it took so much courage for you to be honest with me, and I want you to know how much it means to me that you put my safety ahead of your own interest. I only wish that I could have handled it better." Miklos said, "Of course, it is a difficult situation, Rózsa. But no matter what you decide, I am still glad we met— you know?"

As she watched the plane lift off, everything spun around in her head—here was this absolutely amazing guy: a real gentleman who treated her like a princess, a gifted artist, handsome, made her blood turn to hot melted butter, but… "Okay," she said to herself taking a deep breath, "I just need to get the facts."

When she got home, she called her friend John, a long-time AIDS survivor, whom she had met while serving on an AIDS service board. She asked if she could come over. When she told him what was going on, he said, "Sweetie, there are two answers to your question: the first involves the facts of transmission so you can figure out the best protection available, and the second involves the emotional question—do you want to take the risk? I can help you with the first, but I'm afraid that you're the only one who can decide the second." Maddy loved John for many reasons, but his background as a pastor was her favorite reason: he slipped into a pastoral counseling mode readily and was uncannily good at it. He had been a pastor in a conservative Christian church before he came out as gay—then he was forced out. Another reason she loved him was that he had introduced her to an Episcopal Church in Atlanta which was accepting of gays and had an active AIDS ministry. Her childhood upbringing and experience with church was stiff and judgmental—his church was warm and accepting. She had joined John's church and was even toying with the idea of going to seminary... someday.

John had been exposed to HIV by a partner who did not reveal that he was infected, so John admired Miklos for his courage in being honest. After discussing the complexities of herpes transmission (it is much more easily acquired than HIV and more challenging to protect against), they wrestled together with her feelings about Miklos.

"It's so hard, because it's long distance, you know—I don't even know where the relationship is going at this point; we've only been dating (if you can even call it that) a few months. I've never been in a long-distance relationship before. But I've never met anyone like him—he's fearless; I love that about him; the night we met he charged onto the dance floor with me in tow without saying a word—most straight men don't dance! He moved to this country not knowing anyone or even how he would make a living. But he's also gentle and caring; he listens and remembers things that I've told him. Straight men aren't really known for listening to women, you know?" They both laughed. John was silent for a bit and then said, "I think in the end, your decision should be the emotional one—is this relationship worth it? Do you care enough about him to risk exposure—to take the precautions and protect yourself? It boils down to a decision of the heart." Maddy sighed. "You're right. I guess I just needed to talk it out. You are such a good friend."

The next week, Maddy made an appointment with her gynecologist. To her complete surprise, he said almost the exact same thing that John had told her. "I'm not going to lie to you, Maddy, herpes hits women harder than men—most of them end up in the emergency room on their first outbreak—the pain is so severe. For that reason, in the last two years, they have introduced a female condom, designed to provide additional protection for women against all sexually transmissible diseases but especially herpes, so I can give you a sample. Maddy, I've been your doctor for years now. You should not make a decision like this based on a product; you should make it based on how you feel about this guy."

Driving home, Maddy was hearing the Young Rascals song, "How Can I Be Sure?" playing in her head… "But how do I really know?" she wondered.

CHAPTER THREE

"You're the Best Thing" – Style Council

Maddy phoned Miklos to tell him that she had decided to accept the risk and told him about the box of female condoms she had just bought. They laughed. Miklos said that he had been hired to do some faux finishing at the Atlanta condo of one of the restaurant owners, and the owner wanted it done before Christmas, so Miklos was flying in the weekend before Christmas—arriving Thursday evening and leaving Sunday afternoon, assuming all went well.

The last time Maddy had a man around during Christmas was when she was married, and that seemed eons ago—somehow, she was always single at Christmas. It was great to have someone to help pick out the tree, carry it in and help untangle all the lights. They picked out the tree Friday night, and she decorated it Saturday while he was at work. Her favorite part of Christmas was crafting handmade ornaments, stringing popcorn and cranberries and listening to Christmas music in front of the fireplace.

They had promised each other to just exchange small gifts, so there would not be any awkward pressure. Saturday night, Miklos gave Maddy an angel ornament for the tree that he purchased at the Metropolitan Art Museum Gift Shop in New York, and she gave him a velvet Christmas stocking she had sewn and embroidered that held a mix tape of music that she knew he liked. They slow danced in front of the tree as Maddy's Harry Connick, Jr. CD played, and Maddy thought, "This is the best Christmas I've had in forever."

On Sunday, Maddy took Miklos to the Episcopal Church she had joined, and after the service, he asked her about it. Growing up in a Communist country, he didn't really understand religious practices or faith. Maddy explained, "I was really active in the Presbyterian Church where I was baptized: singing choir, bell choir and church camp in the summers. But as I got older I realized how hypocritical the judgmental attitudes were in that church, and I left. I guess I left God at that point too. But I had an experience about five years ago that changed me. I went on a trip to apartheid South Africa with James, a pastor I knew. He was not there to convert people to Christianity; he was holding intensive sessions with black Christian pastors in Zululand. Under apartheid rule, the native people were taught that the Christian Bible supported the government's segregation and abuse of the native people under apartheid—that it was God's will. The Dutch Afrikaners had taken Bible passages out of context to justify governmental abuse, just as slave owners had done in the United States. The native people had been forced to give up their tribal religions and accept Christianity against their will."

"During the trip I watched as James helped the black pastors to understand that all humans were children of God and loved equally by God. I was amazed as he explained how all forms of loving devotion were holy in God's eyes, and that the tribal customs could be embraced and merged with Christian tradition. I cried as I watched James minister to them with an open heart, with deep compassion and without judgment. It was so beautiful.

When I returned, it took me a long time to find a church in Atlanta like that. But that's what I found in this Episcopal Church—it feels genuinely heart-based. I know that I can bring my whole self here—not just the shiny clean parts. It is a place where I can bring my wounded and struggling parts and be accepted for who I really am—that there is no shame here—that I am loved. It was a real turning point for me when John introduced me to it. Whenever I get overwhelmed, I know I can find peace here."

Miklos said, "When I get stressed, I have Buddhist prayer beads and chants that I say. I use them to calm myself, but I wouldn't say I'm a Buddhist. When I was married, living in New Jersey—they taught me their Buddhist practices, so that's when I started chanting. My mother is very spiritual, though—she practices Reiki. Every time I talk with her on the phone, she says 'let me send you Reiki healing; please accept it.' She says that she can send it anywhere in the world to anyone who accepts it. But I don't really think it works, so I never take her up on it. I guess I don't really believe in anything like that." Maddy had never heard of Reiki before and wanted to know more about it. She was also very curious about Miklos's mother.

They didn't see each other much during the trip because of Miklos's work schedule, but before kissing her goodbye at the airport, he asked Maddy to fly up to New York as soon as she could get some time off. She promised she would. Driving home from the airport, Maddy had one of her favorite Christmas CDs playing, "A Very Special Christmas 2" and when Extreme sang "Christmas Time Again," she smiled and said out loud, "oh, let's _do_ pretend that this feeling will last all year."

CHAPTER FOUR

"I Am the Body Beautiful" – Salt-N-Pepa

Maddy signed up for the "God, Sex and the Body" workshop offered by Gabriel Roth in New York City in March. Her therapist had recommended that Maddy buy Gabriel Roth's CDs, and try dancing her emotions as a way of getting out of her head, where Maddy stayed most of the time. Maddy's mother had been very shut down emotionally and had criticized Maddy whenever she expressed emotions as a child, so as an adult Maddy struggled with identifying her feelings and expressing them. Having taken dance classes since she was in kindergarten, Maddy was very open to the idea of dancing her emotions but felt that she needed a class environment to learn the technique. When she heard about the workshop in New York, she signed up right away. Miklos met Maddy at the Newark airport, where they took a bus from there into the city, and then a cab to the building in Brooklyn where Miklos rented a room in a flat.

On the way to Brooklyn, Miklos explained that when he first arrived in New York from Austria and his visa ran out, he married a woman and got his green card—they lived in New Jersey with her father, but then divorced after several years. He described the special bond that developed between Miklos and his father-in-law, who built Miklos a studio in New Jersey so he could focus on his painting while living there, but Miklos had to give up the studio when he left the marriage. Since then he had been living in a single room in an apartment in Brooklyn which he shared with Christophe, the man who owned it. Christophe accepted paintings in lieu of rent whenever Miklos was short of funds. Fortunately, Miklos was able to rent space from his friend Jakob, who was also a painter, to work on faux finish samples to show clients. Miklos was frustrated, though, not having a space of his own to focus on large canvasses and other projects.

In his room, Maddy was struck by how barren it was in comparison to her house. She wasn't surprised though—one of Miklos's favorite expressions was "rent your shoes if you can." Miklos pulled out a sack full of 35mm slides of the canvasses that he had painted in the New Jersey studio during the '80's. As she held each slide up to the light, Maddy gasped. She had no idea of the depth of his skill—his paintings were ethereal: one canvass had a wispy lace curtain blown by the wind through an open window that was so realistic she could almost feel the wind. Another canvass was a fairy tale scene of a bird in flight carrying lovers through a misty sky, and she felt carried away with it—it was magical! She was awestruck.

A pair of well-worn rollerblades leaned against the closet, and Miklos explained that he was on a speed skating team that practiced at a hockey rink in New Jersey, but that rollerblading was how he cross-trained. He wanted to rollerblade competitively, because New York had competitions that were tiered by age ranges. He said, "The great thing about rollerblading is that it's not hard on your knees like running—there are guys in their 60's blading— that's the way I want to be in twenty years! Would you like to try it?"

They went to Central Park and rented skates for Maddy. After falling on the grass several times, she finally got her balance and tried the pavement. Miklos taught her the wide sweep stroke of a speed skater, which was different from the choppy short strokes that most bladers used. She loved it and promised to get her own set when she got back home. Miklos said, "You must see us speed skate on the ice some time." Maddy promised she would come back in the winter when they were practicing.

The next morning, Maddy attended Gabriel Roth's workshop, and it was amazing! Maddy was stunned at the emotions that came up, as all the attendees paired off and danced opposing archetypes (kind father / brutal father; good mother / bad mother; prince / rogue; virgin / harlot). She found herself laughing, then crying and then surprised at the level of anger that boiled up as she danced—it was as if she could feel all the emotions rushing through her like a wild river. Maddy left the workshop exhausted physically and emotionally, but determined to find more opportunities to explore embodied practices. Dancing added a whole new dimension to her inner work.

The next day, Miklos introduced Maddy to Jakob, the painter who owned the loft where Miklos painted his faux finish samples, and to Stefan, a good friend. Later, Miklos took her to the warehouse where he rented space to practice on his drum set. Maddy giggled, because every man to whom she had been seriously attracted had turned out to be a drummer—even her ex-husband. Miklos said that his favorite music for drumming was jazz; that was why he had so many tapes of Stan Getz, so he could listen to it on his Walkman as he drummed.

In the South Street Seaport, Miklos told her he had something special to show her, and took her to a butterfly gallery called Mariposa. The artist, Marshall Hill, used butterflies bred on farms expressly for the purpose of being encased in Lucite as art. The butterfly displays captivated Maddy, and she bought a small blue butterfly encased in a Lucite cube. Miklos smiled and whispered, "Rózsa, it reminds me of your tattoo!" She said, "You know I got that when I was just 18, but all these years later, it means everything to me—because now it is a symbol of my transformation. That's why I bought this butterfly—it's something I can show everyone, since my tattoo stays hidden!" They laughed.

The entire time Maddy was in New York, they ate out every meal—even breakfast. Maddy was amazed, because she rarely ate out at all back home. And because Miklos had no car, they either used the subway or cabs to get around. Atlanta had a pitiful rapid transit system, because the suburbs fought against its expansion. New

York was definitely a different world than the one in which Maddy lived—and the lifestyle was so different; she silently wondered, could she live in this world? Would she be able to get a job here? How would they afford a place to live? Would their relationship even get to that point or was it all just a romantic fantasy in her head?

When Maddy got back to Atlanta, she bought rollerblades, knee pads and wrist guards and headed off for a business park, where she could practice on Sunday afternoons when no one was there. She heard about the plans for the paving of the Silver Comet Trail close to where she lived in Smyrna, but it was years away from being opened. As she got more experienced, she understood why Miklos loved blading—there was a peaceful calm in the metronome-like swishing back and forth of your legs. She would put on her headphones and listen to "Birds of Fire" by Mahavishnu Orchestra while she bladed—carried off to another dimension. She realized that blading was a form of embodied meditation.

CHAPTER FIVE

"Everybody Hurts" – R.E.M.

Maddy had a conference to attend in Tampa in May, and Miklos surprised her by flying down to be with her. They decided to rent a car and drive to the nearest beach, so they stopped at a drug store to buy suntan lotion and a beach blanket. Maddy turned to look for Miklos in the store, and was puzzled when she finally found him in an aisle that had small stuffed animals. She tried not to even breathe as she quietly watched him take the animals down off the shelf one at a time, holding each close to his chest. It was as though by holding them he could connect to a forgotten part of his childhood. This was a side of him that she had never seen. She tiptoed to another aisle so he didn't know that she had been watching.

Miklos took her dancing that night; then they took a long walk in the moonlight. Maddy told him that she was thinking about leaving her company and going out on her own—one of her friends in Atlanta had just taken a job that required him to travel about nine months out of the year, and he needed someone to share the house and run things while he was gone. If she sold her house, she could move into his, and have her own office—she would need to buy a computer and printer, but she could make it work. Miklos said, "Rózsa, I am so proud of you—you have worked hard, and you should do what makes you happy." Maddy laughed, "Well, you're the one who is inspiring me to step out there and take a chance—I wouldn't even be thinking about taking this step if I had not met someone as fearless as you."

When Maddy returned to Atlanta, she bought a stuffed bear, sewed a rollerblading outfit for it and made tiny rollerblades with cardboard wheels. Then she packaged it up and sent it to Miklos. When he opened the package in Brooklyn, he called Maddy immediately, and she could tell by his voice that he was choked up, but trying to keep his composure. He explained that when he was a small child, he had a teddy bear, a *mackó*, that he slept with and carried everywhere. He had not thought about it in years—until that day in the drugstore. "How—did—*Rózsa*, I didn't see you…" Maddy confessed that she had seen him in the aisle with stuffed animals at the drug store but sensed that it was a private moment, so she didn't want to intrude. She explained that she bought the bear and made the outfit for it when she got home. Maddy hung up the phone, struck by the depth of emotions that welled up in Miklos. She remembered a scene from the movie "Camelot" before Vanessa Redgrave discovered that Richard Harris was the king—he showed such vulnerability and emotions telling her the story of when he was a small child and met Merlin the magician.

CHAPTER SIX

"Just Around the Corner to the Light of Day" – Joan Jett

Energized by the Gabriel Roth workshop, Maddy sought out more workshops—she signed up for a "Women's Renewal" retreat led by Gloria Karpinski after her therapist recommended that she read "Where Two Worlds Touch." The focus of the workshop was inner transformation—how one must make a commitment to transform oneself. So much at the workshop was new to Maddy: the Goddess Kuan Yin who embodied compassion and mercy; the Great Mother meditation; guided visualizations; and the seven chakras (energy centers) of the body through which Qi, the life force energy moved. She was amazed to learn that each of the seven chakras in the body was associated with a different type of psychological wound that frequently showed up in a physical ailment in that body region. She couldn't wait to talk with her therapist about this. She learned that Reiki was one of many different spiritual practices for moving Qi through the body. Maddy immediately thought of Miklos's mother and wished that she could have attended the "Women's Renewal" workshop with her.

One of the first exercises at Gloria Karpinski's workshop was entering a small room in which the walls were covered with postcards and pictures of women portrayed in different settings. The participants were instructed to grab the first two pictures that spoke to them—without giving it any thought. Maddy first grabbed a photo of a young girl in a heated argument with an older woman. The next picture she grabbed was of a woman strapped to a water wheel being tortured. Tears welled up in Maddy's eyes as she looked at the sad pictures that rang so true for her. Her childhood had been tough, the only child of a single workaholic mother who showed no emotion—she would not even hug Maddy. Their arguments were never resolved, there was no buffer, and the household was always tense. It was more like being raised by a caveman than by a woman, and Maddy had no role model for holding both feminine and masculine energies. Staring at the waterwheel, she thought of her mother who told her that life and work were a struggle— that you simply had to "tough it out" till retirement. Maddy had always told herself that she would be different—but here was the waterwheel, telling her that her career was not so different from her mother's after all. Maddy realized that most of her working life she had been trying to out-man-the-men (just as her mother had done); she had been afraid of her femininity—afraid to show weakness—afraid to be vulnerable. But now there was a new energy, thanks to Miklos. It was his demonstration of vulnerability that was empowering her to explore hers. It was time to tear down more walls and unearth her inner feminine—time to find a way to balance yin and yang. Maybe now that she would be setting up her own business, it might be possible to even find that balance in work....

Back in Atlanta after the workshop, the monthly Episcopal Church newsletter featured an article on a new book "The Heart Aroused: Poetry and the Preservation of the Soul in Corporate America," by David Whyte. Maddy saw it as a sign that she was on the right track—finally. She went to a bookstore and bought it. Maybe she could find a way to introduce this into her management consulting?

In July, Maddy sold her home in Smyrna, put most of her belongings in storage, and moved into a house sharing arrangement with Sam, an engineer who traveled almost nine months out of the year; she would pay him rent and look after things when he was away. She also reached an agreement with her company that would allow her leave and launch her own consulting business.

Over the summer, Maddy set up a room in Sam's house for an office; she purchased her first personal computer and printer, signed up for a block of classes on computer skills, and took a class on how to start a business. She got a business license and worked on different layouts for a marketing brochure.

In September, Miklos was hired to do a job in Chattanooga, and Maddy drove up to stay with him. He asked her to go to Budapest to meet his family for Christmas. He explained that it was complicated, because he was estranged from his father, who was a true believer in Communism. When Miklos escaped to Austria, his father called him a traitor and told Miklos that he hoped he would be shot by the border guards. Maddy was horrified at the thought of this. "But you will love my mother," he assured her, "If I give you her address, would you write to her? She would love that." Maddy said, "Of course I will."

On the drive back to Atlanta, Maddy had a vision of a quilt that she wanted to sew. She had seen photographs transferred onto fabric at an art shop back home. She could have the art shop transfer onto fabric photos of Miklos and his sister, Korinna, and also transfer onto fabric some of the slides of the canvasses he had painted. She could even attach the pictures of his art with Velcro, so that each year, she could send new fabric photos of for his parents to attach! The center of the quilt would be an appliqued fabric tree; she would embroider his parents' initials into the base of the tree; the branches would bear the photos of their two children, and all along the edges of the tree would be photos of the canvasses Miklos painted—so the quilt would show both the literal and the figurative fruit of the family tree. She had an idea for the center of the quilt: a piece of embroidery that said, "A loving and nurturing tree bears beautiful fruit." The challenge would be embroidering it in a different language: Hungarian!

All Maddy's projects came to her as visions (clairvoyance); she had been sewing large concept quilts for over a decade—always as gifts for other people (on a marriage, a birthday, for someone who was very ill, etc.).

Fortunately, at Sam's house, she would have the space to work on it! She got busy right away.

She had another idea as well: a few weeks ago, in a bookstore, Maddy noticed a memory book—a spiral bound book with lots of lines and space to be completed by a parent or grandparent, writing in their memories about different phases of their life, tracking three generations of memories (grandparents, parents and children). Maddy decided to use her new computer skills to create her personalized versions: one memory book for Emil, Miklos's father, and one for Zsófia, his mother. "Who knows?" She thought, "Maybe his father would be able to write the love he felt but could not say to Miklos?" Maddy sent the personalized memory books to Zsófia, explaining what they were and why she was sending them. Maddy asked her if she could please keep them a surprise so that Miklos did not know about them. She asked Zsófia to try to have them completed by Christmas, so they could give them to Miklos as a present. Zsófia wrote back that she loved the idea and promised that the books would be filled out by Christmas.

The weeks flew by as Maddy was immersed in sewing the quilt. And as she saw the tree coming together on it, she could hear Rod Stewart singing, "Every picture tells a story don't it?" And she shook her head in amazement.

CHAPTER SEVEN

"Love is a Rose" – Neil Young

Maddy was working on the quilt until the week she left for New York, and when she finished, she was so proud of it. It was 6 feet round and designed to hang on a wall. She rolled the quilt up into a laundry bag and then stuffed that into a sleeping bag sack so she could check it through at the airport.

When Miklos met Maddy at the airport, she immediately sensed that something was wrong, but she couldn't put her finger on it. Miklos seemed nervous, tense and preoccupied. As soon as they arrived at his room in

Brooklyn, he left, telling Maddy that he had a painting job and then was attending a Knicks game afterward with this friends. Alone in his room, Maddy was confused and felt lost. What had happened since Chattanooga? Was he regretting having asked her to go to Budapest? Should she just get on a plane and go back to Atlanta?

When he finally came home, Maddy mustered her courage and said, "Babe, something is bothering you—please just talk to me!" Miklos, blurted out, "Well, I was at a party last week and they were talking about relationships. I said that I didn't see myself in a relationship; I didn't see myself with anyone long-term—I didn't need anyone and was perfectly content on my own. But this guy said, 'Hey, you've got a girlfriend! And you're taking her home to meet your parents. I thought you two were getting serious.' But I said 'No, I just thought they would really like each other, and it's been such a long time since I've been back there—it just seemed like a good idea.' "

Maddy felt all the blood rush out of her face and her stomach drop; she was stunned. It was true that they had never talked about marriage, but they had been dating a little over a year, so she thought the subject might come up at some point. This was not at all what she was expecting. She sat down on the bed, staring at the carpet and tried to collect her thoughts. Miklos was still standing by the door, uncomfortably shifting his weight from one foot to the other.

After some time, Maddy looked up at Miklos and said, "I want you to know that I did not have any hidden agenda for this trip; but I did intend to have a talk with you in another month or two about where we are going. Because if we weren't getting to a deeper level after dating for a year and half, I was going to call it quits. Now that you've brought it up, and you say you've made up your mind, there's no reason for me to wait. When we return from Budapest, that's it—I will be breaking up with you."

Miklos's jaw dropped; he was genuinely shocked. "What?" Maddy took a deep breath and said, "Babe, I turn 41 next year, and I'm at a point in my life where I am ready to go for more: professionally, personally, emotionally, spiritually—more in every part of my life—I want it all, and I'm willing to hold out—to wait for it. Miklos, you're an amazing man, and you know that I love you—I wouldn't trade anything for the time we've been together. Without you, I would never have had the courage to leave my company and start out on my own—you have changed me in so many ways. I have absolutely no regrets. But as much as I love you, I know if I stay any longer, I'll end up resentful and angry, because I want more—and you don't."

Miklos stood silent. As he looked at her, a wave of heartbreak seemed to cross over his eyes, because he realized that she was determined about this. He stubbornly asked, "But why can't things just stay the way they are?" Maddy studied his face for a while and said, "There was a time in my life when my self-esteem was so low, that I would have stayed with a man who wouldn't commit to me. But I have worked very hard in therapy and I am beginning to tear down inner walls and face the wounds inside them; I am slowly learning how to nurture myself. I've got a lot of work ahead of me, but I'm finally ready to open my heart and my life to someone. I know I deserve someone to love me, to commit to me, so we can work together to build a real relationship. So that's why it can't stay the way it is."

Quickly, Miklos said, "Well, I have no use for therapy." Maddy smiled and said, "Your walls are your protection, your safety—believe me, I know. But walls isolate—and there is so much pain inside them. For me, the pain of being isolated behind those walls became greater than the pain of tearing them down. That was when I got into therapy—at that point I knew I didn't have a choice." Miklos was silent.

All this time Maddy had been stoic, but the reality of it all was hitting her, and she was choking back tears now. "If this is too hard, I can change my plane reservation and fly back to Atlanta tomorrow instead of going with you to Budapest, but I wish that you would still take the quilt to your parents." "No," Miklos almost shouted, "No, you <u>must</u> go—my parents are expecting you; they are counting on you being there—you <u>must</u> come." "Okay. Okay. Then I will go with you. But you understand, after that, it's over?" Miklos looked down at the carpet and muttered, "Yes, all right. I understand."

CHAPTER EIGHT

"Budapest" – George Ezra

They sat in traffic for two hours trying to get to Kennedy Airport; when they finally arrived, the place was a madhouse—the crowds were spilling out onto the sidewalk. They didn't board their flight until an hour after its scheduled departure time, and then had to wait behind 43 other planes to take off. Due to all the delays, they missed their connection in London and waited in the wrong line to change the tickets, which meant they had another hour delay. There was a woman alone sobbing in the line in front of them, and Maddy went to comfort her. She spoke broken English but told Maddy that her sister was very sick, and she was worried that she wouldn't get to her in time to say their goodbyes. When Maddy returned to stand next to Miklos, he said, "What a stupid woman—as if crying will make this line go any faster." Maddy was shocked. She had never seen this side of Miklos—so crass and uncaring. It was as if a different personality had taken over him. She said, "Babe, her sister is dying, and she may not get home in time to see her before she passes—and she is all alone and afraid. Have a heart. Show some compassion." Miklos crossed his arms, shrugged and was silent. Maddy wondered if Miklos was raising his inner walls as a protection against heartbreak: if he could steel himself to a stranger's pain, maybe he could steel himself against the pain of losing Maddy....

When they arrived in Budapest, their luggage was still in London, but Miklos's parents were there to meet them. Zsófia put her arms around Maddy immediately and was just as warm and loving as her letters. But inside, Maddy was wrestling with a tumble of emotions: feeling estranged from Miklos while at the same time feeling an instant kinship with his mother. His father Emil was reserved but outwardly warm and friendly. Maddy could feel tension between Emil and Miklos, but could also see that they were trying to get along. Fortunately, Zsófia spoke English, but Miklos still had to translate for his father, Emil, and his sister, Korinna.

When they arrived at Miklos's parents' apartment, it was an adjustment. The heat was so dry that their throats became sore and parched by the next morning. There was not enough hot water for a shower or a bath, so they squatted in the cold tub, only turning the water on to lather and rinse. It was bitter cold. Maddy wore tights under her jeans and '80's leggings over her jeans, double socks, double gloves, a ski mask and several layers of sweaters under her ski jacket. The public buildings they visited were not heated and neither were churches. Within three days, both Miklos and Maddy were sick. She had packed a course of antibiotics and sinus medication, but was still very weak.

Aside from being ill, Maddy was in awe of Budapest—the sheer beauty of it—everywhere she looked she saw art, murals, statues, carvings and churches built long before the Russian occupation, each more beautiful than the next. As they walked along the Danube River, she felt as though she had entered a fairy tale land. She understood how Miklos's talent was sparked in such a place, but she also understood why he would need freedom to explore and express it outside of the repressive Communist state.

On Christmas, his parents presented Miklos with the memory books they had completed for him. His father, who once believed that the border guards should shoot Miklos for escaping to the West, had written 43 pages of memories in a single day! He also prepared a collage of photos of Miklos—some of which Miklos did not even remember. It was so clear to Maddy, seeing the family united again, that she had a greater purpose in his life than being a lover.

Then, Maddy brought out the quilt. Zsófia and Emil were astonished. Maddy explained to them that lovers often carve their initials into a tree, and that was why their initials were embroidered on a heart applique on the tree in the quilt. She told them that Miklos had helped her with the translation into Hungarian of the phrase, "A loving and nurturing tree bears beautiful fruit." On either side of that square were fabric photos of Miklos and his sister Korinna. They had never seen the images of the painted canvasses that were transferred into fabric around the edges of the trees. Emil proudly hung the quilt up in the room that Miklos and Korinna shared growing up. It was a powerful experience, and Maddy knew that it was all meant to be.

In the week between Christmas and New Year's Eve, Miklos walked Maddy through each phase of his life in Budapest: the hospital where he was born, each apartment where they lived, his nursery school, kindergarten, elementary and high school, the Hungarian Academy of Fine Arts, where he honed his craft and where he studied stage design; he even showed her the nightclubs in which he had been too rowdy and had been thrown out.

Again, Maddy was a tumble of emotions: here she was, getting closer to him in understanding his background while at the same time preparing to leave him. Her heart felt ripped apart, and she desperately wanted to escape— just go back to Atlanta—but she knew that it was important for her to stay.

The next day they boarded a train to Eger, a mountain resort town where his uncle lived. It was just as beautiful as Budapest, but the best part for Miklos and Maddy was that his uncle's condominium had hot showers and less abrasive heat. Perhaps it was because they were more comfortable, that Maddy decided to tell Miklos a story about a man in one of her computer classes back home who wondered why he backed away from commitment to a woman he loved. "I told him that a real relationship with a woman is just like the business that he ran so successfully: it takes vision, dedication and a willingness to work on it every day. Until he was ready to give that to the relationship, he would continue to back away." Miklos said, "That man is so much farther along than I am—I don't even think about it." Maddy was wishing that this was all a bad dream, but knew she had to "stay present" as her therapist would say.

The next day, Miklos told Maddy about his past relationships—how in his mind, they had been a means to an end: one to get into Austria, one to get a green card in America and one to get farther along in the art world in

America. He had never really opened up his heart to any of those women. Then he explained that he had shut down his heart after it was broken in high school by a woman he thought he would marry and spend the rest of his life with—when she left him, he decided "Never again." Maddy was silent a while, and then said, "My mother was a workaholic who built solid walls around herself—she never even let anyone hug her. I think if there had been sperm banks back in the 1950's, she would never have married at all—as it was, she threw my father out shortly after I was born. I had no model for opening my heart, no model for love and no model for how relationships worked. I was a complete mess until I got into therapy a few years ago, believe me. When I was in college, a guy I knew told me I was "plastic". It was devastating, because I had no idea how hard and cold I was—like plastic—how I had built walls around my heart just like my mother despite every effort to be different. But now I'm trying to get less "plastic": to get in touch with my fears, my wounds—my baggage. I think a real relationship is about working through pain together, to find ways of growing together." Now Miklos was silent. "You are much farther along than I am—I don't even see the need to work at anything."

The depth of the chasm between them was starting to sink in. Maddy decided that the only way to get through this experience was to let it go and be content with being a tourist in a magical land. They went to the medieval Castle of Eger and walked around the town. On New Year's Eve, they went to a medieval wine cellar that had been converted into a dance club. Maddy and Miklos danced for two solid hours—and would have danced longer, but someone poured champagne on them! Everyone was setting fireworks off outside and spraying champagne—it was insane!

When it was time to go to the airport, Zsófia cried and thanked Maddy for being with Miklos. Emil was choked up—he could not speak, but embraced Miklos and Maddy warmly. She had said nothing to Zsófia about what was really going on, but something in Zsófia's eyes told her that she was aware that there was trouble in paradise. Maddy resolved to write her a long letter when she got back to Atlanta.

After arriving in Brooklyn, Maddy and Miklos slept almost the entire day. The next night, Maddy went with Miklos to the skating rink in New Jersey, where she watched his team whip across the ice effortlessly. It was mesmerizing. As she watched, Joni Mitchell's "Coyote" was playing in her head... no regrets, Miklos, you just picked up a hitchhiker—and I'll be getting out... a bit up the road...

At the airport, Maddy was fighting back her tears; she said, "Call me if you decide you want to tear down your walls." Staring out the window in the plane, she heard Laura Nyro singing "The Bells." No, she would never hear them again.

CHAPTER NINE

"Do the Walls Come Down" – Carly Simon

Maddy threw herself into her business as a refuge from her grief. Eventually, she wrote Zsófia a long letter thanking her for everything and explaining what happened in the relationship with her son. To her surprise, Zsófia wrote back, saying that she had known in her heart the situation already, but was deeply grateful for Maddy being in Miklos's life—for reuniting Emil and Miklos through the memory books, and for the quilt. She called Maddy an angel sent by God to help their family, and no matter what happened she wanted Maddy to promise to always be in touch with her, because Maddy was now part of their family. Reading the letter, Maddy's hands shook and she sobbed, because she realized that Zsófia had become more of a true mother figure to her in a matter of a few months than her own mother had ever been to her in 40 years.

Her therapist recommended that she read, "When the Heart Waits" by Sue Monk Kidd. Maddy read it twice, underlining her favorite passages and writing in the margins of the book. It was a perfect roadmap of the combined spiritual and inner growth that Maddy was undertaking. Her favorite line was, "we have to trust that our sacred hearts really do have wings." Oh, but entering into that trust was difficult.

At the Episcopal Church she attended, she learned about a walking meditation called a labyrinth that was in Chartres Cathedral in France. Maddy immediately felt a call to walk it. An Episcopal priest in San Francisco, The Reverend Lauren Artress, had researched it and introduced it to Grace Cathedral. Now, she was bringing a 40-foot circular canvass replica of the labyrinth to churches around the country to inspire them to create their own. In her workshop, Ms. Artress explained that there were three steps to walking the labyrinth: (1) unburdening yourself of a problem you had been trying to carry alone (the walk in); (2) finding insight or illumination into your burdens in the center of the labyrinth; (3) walking out in union with Spirit finding comfort and release. After attending the workshop, Maddy journaled about all that had happened in the last year and how she needed some guidance in finding a way forward, because she felt so lost. On the labyrinth walk, Maddy felt a strong presence of Spirit and heard an inner voice telling her that she needed to be patient with herself, that she was only seeing a small part of a bigger picture and that she would soon see why everything was happening as it should. She sat down afterward, a bit disoriented. She knew that she had experienced a very real presence, but she had never experienced "clairaudience" before—and had no idea what was meant by the message she heard.

She had been reading about spirituality in the workplace and talked about it with the rector of the Episcopal Church she attended. He gave her a brochure from the seminary he had attended and encouraged her to contact them, because they were doing groundbreaking work in that area. She wrote them and learned that they were offering a conference on it. Maddy registered for it right away and wondered if she was really meant to attend seminary—maybe that was the "bigger picture" in all of this.

Her therapist introduced her to the works of Robert Johnson, who wrote small, easy-to-read books on Jungian psychology. She raced through "He," "She," "We", "Inner Work," and "Transformation;" but when she reached "Owning Your Shadow: Understanding the Dark Side of the Psyche," she knew this was work that both

Miklos and she needed to tackle. She wrote Miklos a long letter about everything she had been reading and the work she was doing with her therapist. "I thought you were a lover, but you were a teacher. You taught me to open up to feminine energy and its healing power. You taught me risk-taking and living in the moment. You taught me that a man could be very affectionate and tender. Your lessons were as powerful as your lovemaking and both will stay in my heart forever. Whenever I think of the first man I truly opened my heart to—make no mistake—it will be you."

In the letter, Maddy assured him that she was not encouraging him to open up out of a selfish desire just to "get a man back the way I want him," because "the only thing certain about the journey of self-discovery is that the outcome is uncertain! When the outer shell of the persona is shattered, and layer by layer of protective coverings removed, the true essence of the person is completely new—it quite often bears no resemblance to what came before." So Maddy promised Miklos that she was releasing any hope for a future in which they would be together— that she only wanted the best possible outcome for him as an individual. She folded the letter inside a copy of the "Owning Your Shadow". She closed the letter with a quote from 1 Corinthians 13: "Love never fails....And now these three things remain: faith, hope and love. But the greatest of these is love."

About a week later, Miklos phoned Maddy, and they talked for an hour—he had started reading the book, but wasn't really sure he was ready for what Robert Johnson was saying. Maddy said, "Just sit with it then. Take your time. How is work going?" He told her that he had been working on a friend's computer creating art digitally—how one of the designs he created was going to be on a book cover! He felt stuck though: he wanted his own equipment, and he wanted to be able to truly study digital art in a professional school that could train him properly—just as he had studied back in Budapest when he was trained to use traditional media. His frustration lay in his inability to see a way to finance everything. Computers, software, and education all seemed like pieces of an unattainable pipe dream when he was making so little money painting walls. Maddy suggested that he form a limited liability corporation. She had learned about them when she was exploring options for setting up her management consulting business. She explained how it worked, and asked Miklos why all the people he knew from the '80's when he sold large canvasses couldn't be investors in an LLC? Miklos sighed. "That was a long time ago—I'm sure they have forgotten me, and I have lost touch with them anyway." Maddy promised to try to think of other ideas. She said, "You and I are both going through a time of uncertainty—I am trying to start a new business, and you are trying to get into a different one. All I can tell you is what helps me—and that is knowing that I am never alone in all this—because I feel the presence of God." Miklos was quiet for some time and then said, "I just wish I had your faith." After they hung up, Maddy closed her eyes and prayed that he would be all right; she was worried about his dark mood and his limited support network, but she knew she had to let go—she had to let him find his own way.

John asked Maddy to create a panel for the Names Project AIDS Quilt for his partner who died of AIDS before Maddy met John. He wanted to be able to see the panel displayed with the full Names Project Quilt at the National Mall in October that year. In a way, sewing the quilt panel allowed Maddy to share in her grief work with John, as she sewed and he provided creative input for the panel design. After it was finished, John took Maddy to a friend's beach house near Savannah, and they spent hours walking the beach arm-in-arm and confiding in one another. "Honestly, it feels as though I have never been through a breakup before because my heart wasn't really open before—it is just so raw and exposed now," Maddy told him. "I know, sweetie—it's like when I first came out as gay—it's devastating to risk opening yourself, to be truly vulnerable—only to watch your dream crumble. But you must not let this heartbreak close you down again. What if I had done that? I would never have met the wonderful man I am in love with now," John said, hugging her.

In April, Maddy's therapist told her about an organization called "Journey Into Wholeness" that was based in Brevard, North Carolina and had been founded by Annette Cullipher, whom her therapist knew. Maddy contacted them, and they sent her a brochure about a conference in May where Robert Johnson would be one of the speakers! Maddy knew that she was meant to be there when she read the prayer of an Anglican bishop, George Appleton, featured on the brochure: "Give Me a Candle of the Spirit, O God":

Give me a candle of the Spirit, O God
As I go down into the deep of my own being.
Show me the hidden things.
Take me down to the spring of my life,
And tell me my nature and my name.
Give me freedom to grow, so that I may become
My true self – the fulfillment of the seed
Which You planted in me at my making.
Out of the deep I cry unto thee, O God.
Amen.

On the way to the conference, Maddy was hearing The Waterboys "The Pan Within" playing in her head— she was certainly on a journey deep under the skin and had no idea where it would lead. At the conference, there was Tai Ji every day (an opportunity for body work) and a

Eucharist offered by an Episcopal priest (an opportunity for spiritual work) prior to the lectures on inner work. Maddy heard Robert Johnson, June Singer (whose book "Boundaries of the Soul" was one of Maddy's favorites), and Ian Baker (whom she had not read). She was introduced to the art of mandalas by Susan Fincher (a form of art therapy), and Maddy was surprised to learn that Ms. Fincher was from Atlanta! Whenever she would tell anyone at the conference about her work and her interest in spirituality in the workplace, she would hear the same thing, "You should go to seminary!" The message of the labyrinth kept tapping her on the shoulder—was this the "bigger picture"?

As Maddy drove back to Atlanta after the conference, she was hearing the song by Sting, "Fortress Around Your Heart" playing in her head. She wondered how many land mines she had laid, how many walls she had erected against people and situations in her life—and what it would take to set all her "battlements on fire".

CHAPTER TEN

"Gangsta's Paradise" – Coolio

Miklos had been calling Maddy about once a week for months, not talking long, saying he just wanted to hear her voice. But after the first week in August, his calls stopped. Maddy left messages on his machine, but worried when the recording said that it was full and not accepting any more messages. Meanwhile, Maddy was being haunted by a song, "Gangsta's Paradise" that played in her head so much that she stopped at a record store to get the CD of soundtrack from the movie "Dangerous Minds". She played the CD in her car and in her room in Sam's house; she spent hours going over the lyrics for a clue as to why it was possessing her.

When she picked up John to take him to an AIDS service organization meeting, he looked puzzled and asked, "Okay, Maddy, when did you start listening to Coolio?" Maddy shook her head, and said, "John, it's the craziest thing! I've never been haunted by a song before— it's like I can't get away from it—it plays in my head all day and all night." John said, "What do you think it means?" "Honestly, I have no idea—I keep turning the words over and over in my head—money and power, guns, danger—and that choir in the background. It all feels so ominous, like I'm being given a warning about death, but none of it makes any sense!" John said, "Sweetie, I'm worried about you. What can I do?" Maddy said, "I don't know—I'm worried too—either I'm completely losing my mind or something awful is about to happen, and I don't know what it is or who is in danger."

Maddy was working on a manual for one of her clients, and they were using a publishing company in New York City. They had been frustrated with faxing revisions back and forth, so Maddy had been thinking about flying up to oversee the final edits in person—but because it would involve a trip to New York, Maddy was struggling; it was a complicated decision.

On Friday, August 23rd, Maddy came home to three frantic messages on her answering machine: the first was Christophe, who rented the room to Miklos. He had not seen Miklos since Monday, August 5th and asked if there was any way Maddy could fly to Brooklyn to help him figure out what was going on. The second was Stefan, the close friend of Miklos whom Maddy had met, saying the same thing—he said that Miklos had been excited about getting samples of digital art out to the list of companies that Maddy had sent him, but was depressed about money. Then suddenly he had just disappeared.

The third call was odd—it was from Carl, a man whom Maddy had never even met—she knew his name because Miklos mentioned him as a skating buddy—she wondered how Carl would have found her telephone number. His message was similar to the other two, except Carl said that the last time he saw Miklos he asked Carl where he could get a gun for protection.

Maddy returned Christophe's call first and arranged to stay with him; then she booked a flight leaving that same night—the travel agent asked "and when will you be returning?" Maddy froze. How long does it take to solve a disappearance of someone you love? Maddy snapped back to reality and answered, "Uh, I'm not really sure—how about a departure at noon on Monday and then I can change it if I need to?" She then called Stefan and Carl and told them she would touch base after she arrived. It suddenly occurred to her that she could finalize the manual while she was in New York, so she called the publishing company and explained that the trip was unexpected and she would let them know her availability when she got there.

On the plane, the businessman seated next to Maddy casually asked her if her trip to New York was for business or pleasure; she suddenly heard herself telling him that she was going to New York to identify a body. It was as though someone else was speaking through her—she had never had the experience of channeling before. He immediately opened his briefcase and pretended to work. She stared out the window, uneasy with what had just happened.

She arrived at Newark Airport a little after midnight, called Christophe from a pay phone, took a bus into the city and then took a cab to Brooklyn. Christophe had a pot of tea and some cookies waiting for her; they sat down and went over everything Christophe knew. He said that he had gone into Miklos's room, listened to the messages on Miklos's answering machine and written down all the telephone numbers that were recorded on the caller ID unit attached to his phone. Then, Christophe called the telephone numbers that he did not recognize. All the calls and numbers were either painting jobs, Miklos's friends, or Maddy—except for one that puzzled him. He said that when he called one number, the guy who answered it had a very gruff voice, muttered something about a Russian Airline and then demanded to know what

Christophe wanted. "I told him I must have dialed a wrong number and hung up, but Maddy, that was no airline."

Maddy walked into Miklos's room and had to catch herself: he had pictures of her everywhere—the rollerblading bear was propped up against one of them, the mix tapes she had sent him were stacked next to his tape player and the Robert Johnson book she had sent him was on his desk. It was as if nothing had changed in their relationship. She sat down on his bed, and the reality of what was ahead of her suddenly hit her. It wasn't Coolio any more that was playing in her head—now it was Peter Gabriel's "In Your Eyes." Had the time with Maddy kept Miklos "awake and alive"? Is that why he kept her alive in his room through her pictures? What had happened in the time that they had been apart?

She went to sleep in his bed praying for answers.

CHAPTER
ELEVEN

"Three Strange Days" – School of Fish

When she woke up, Christophe had bagels, cream cheese and fruit for her and they talked about how to begin. She realized how lucky she was that Miklos lived with him. Spreading Miklos's mail out on the floor: she looked over his credit card statements and telephone bill. Christophe helped her as they started calling hospitals in Brooklyn, looking for an admission on or around August 5th. One of the hospitals told them that if they filed a Missing Persons report, the police would handle the hospitals. They also got the number for the morgue, so

Maddy phoned them. The staff member said that they had a "floater" John Doe that was pulled from the Hudson River bank just below the George Washington Bridge on August 9th. The body was badly decomposed and would require dental records to identify—but generally fit Miklos's description. The staff member was puzzled though, explaining that a body doesn't decompose that rapidly being in water for four days—the water would have preserved it. A chill went through Maddy as she remembered the words that came out of her mouth on the airplane while talking to the businessman seated next to her.

Maddy called Missing Persons and made an appointment to meet with Detective Seward at 3 p.m. to fill out an information report. Detective Seward did a John Doe search of area hospitals, but found nothing. He gave her the telephone number for the jail at Ryker's Island, but was told they had no one by the name Miklos Takács. Maddy called Stefan and explained what she had been told; Stefan agreed to go with Maddy to the police station.

While she was waiting on Stefan, Maddy decided to check for activity on Miklos's credit cards—but she needed his Social Security number. She found it in his tax files; when she called the credit card companies, she was told that there was no activity after August 5th. She called his bank, and the same was true for his accounts there. Looking further in Miklos's files, she found paystubs from a catering company, and remembered that Miklos used to work there to earn extra money—she would contact them later to see if they had heard from him.

Next, Maddy called the woman who had left multiple frantic calls on Miklos's answering machine about a painting job on the Upper East Side that was scheduled to start on August 6th. Miklos had failed to call her as promised on the evening of August 5th to confirm. Maddy explained that something terrible had happened and that Maddy was sorry, but that the woman would have to retain the services of another painter. Suddenly, Maddy flashed on a conversation in which Miklos had explained why he had such difficulty finding people whom he could trust to work for him on his painting projects. "They say they will show up and then they don't—they have no work ethic. I have no respect for that. I am a man of my word: if I say I will be there at 8 a.m., then I am there—and not at 8:30 or the next day." Miklos would not simply abandon a job without a word. What could have happened?

Searching for answers, Maddy called Jakob, who had the loft where Miklos rented space to work on painting samples. Jakob told her that he had seen Miklos on August 5th at about 1:30 p.m. Jakob was just returning from a painting job and found Miklos working on a painting sample. Maddy asked him what they talked about, and Jakob said, "All I remember is that Miklos said he had a lot going on, but wouldn't say more." Maddy asked him what Miklos was wearing; after a minute, Jakob said, "Let me think, a white t-shirt, khaki shorts, white socks and his construction boots."

Next she called Daniel at the catering company, told him that Miklos had disappeared and asked when he had last talked with Miklos. He said that it had been a few weeks ago, that they had gone together to the bank. He remembered that Miklos asked him if he knew anyone who could get him a gun. Daniel asked him why he needed a gun all of a sudden, and was surprised when Miklos answered by saying that he carried a lot of cash. Daniel said, "Maddy, I know how much his jobs pay—and how much I pay—so I asked, 'What's a lot of cash?' but he didn't answer. I thought it was odd. I told him that the place to start was with a gun license—he would need that first." Daniel asked her to please let him know if she found out anything; she promised she would. Maddy remembered the message that Carl left on her answering machine back in Atlanta—about Miklos asking where he could get a gun. What was all this about?

Maddy went through Miklos's desk drawers and his trash can. She found his passport, but then something caught her eye: it was an envelope from the National Rifle Association postmarked July 29th. It contained a brochure on New York gun laws and a computer printout of research on gun laws. Then she found a receipt from a gun shop for a gun license that read "for home protection pistol." So Miklos had followed Daniel's advice—but why did Miklos suddenly need a gun?

Then, she found his checkbook—it had carbon copies of all the checks he had written. The last carbon showed a check written to an art school with the memo, "digital design winter 1997." It was dated August 5th. Miklos must have mailed it the morning he disappeared. So he was going for his dream after all—but where was he suddenly getting the money for school? What was he doing to get the money? Was it the reason he needed a gun all of a sudden? Maddy's head was spinning.

Under the checkbook was a receipt for the rental of a red Ford Explorer from July 15th to July 16th. "Where was he going?" Maddy wondered. She checked the phone bill, and it showed that he had called in for messages on July 16th. Maddy called that number and it was a phone booth in the Hudson Valley about an hour and a half away from the city. She called Daniel and asked him if Miklos was working out there on a catering job, but Daniel said "No, I didn't have any jobs that week for Miklos—and no work up in that area at all."

So Maddy called the car rental company and said, "You rented a car to Miklos Takács" and was immediately interrupted by the man who answered the phone. "Where is that guy? I want to talk to him. Did you get my message?" Maddy was startled and replied, "No, the answering machine is full, and messages haven't been recorded in some time." He said, "Well, all I know is that guy left my car on the George Washington Bridge, and it's being towed into our garage right now." Maddy was confused, "What car did he rent and when?" "He rented a silver Ford Escort on August 5th at 10:30 a.m. for a rental of 1000 miles/wk through August 23rd for $289/wk." Maddy said, "If I come right now, can I see the car?" He said, "Yes, but I'm closing pretty soon." She said, "I'm on my way." Maddy hung up the phone but thought, "Wait. It's 2:30 p.m. on a Saturday afternoon—why would a car rental place be closing?"

Maddy called Detective Seward, told him about the car rental she had discovered and cancelled her 3:00 meeting with him. He asked her to call him from the rental place and tell him what she found out. Just then, Stefan walked in, and she explained to him that there was a change of plans.

CHAPTER TWELVE

"Beware of Darkness" – Leon Russell

Maddy and Stefan took a cab to the car rental company, and when they arrived, the silver Ford Escort was sitting in the garage. The doors were locked, but she could see a plastic water bottle that was mostly empty next to Miklos's backpack, a white plastic grocery store bag, wrappers from a sandwich, a copy of the New York Times folded under his backpack and Miklos's blue jean jacket. The attendant told them he didn't have keys to the car (which sounded odd to Maddy), so Stefan walked from the garage into the car rental office to call Detective Seward.

Maddy closed her eyes and immediately had a vision: she saw Miklos get out of the car to meet several men, but then there was an altercation and they dragged Miklos away. She didn't tell anyone about her vision, but when Stefan returned he said, "You're really pale, Maddy, are you all right? Do you need to sit down?" She said, "Yes, let's just get his things and go." The attendant opened the car and gave all the personal belongings in it to Maddy.

They took a cab to the apartment that Stefan shared with his girlfriend. Maddy threw water on her face and sat down, still in shock. They looked through the backpack and found Miklos's Day-Timer, address book, Buddhist prayer bead pouch and some tools for fixing his rollerblades. Maddy shook her head, "Why was the car on the George Washington Bridge? You know that is where the morgue said that the floater was found—right under it." Stefan said, "It doesn't make any sense. My buddies and I parachute off that bridge. I told Miklos about it—told him it was a real adrenaline rush, but he thought we were crazy and refused to try it. The parachuting gets expensive though, because it is illegal. The New York Port Authority is located right next to the bridge, so they film it 24 hours a day, monitoring it for jumpers. We get arrested pretty often and fined for illegal parachuting. Maddy, you know after so many jumps and so many arrests, I've made some friends at the Port Authority. Why don't I call them and ask if their tapes show any jumpers between August 5th and August 9th?" Stefan made the call, and his friend said he would check the videotape. Later, the phone rang, and the friend said that there was no record of any jumpers any time between August 5th and August 9th. Stefan looked at Maddy and said, "I don't know why that car was on the bridge, but I don't believe for a minute that Miklos jumped." Maddy closed her eyes and said, "Neither do I."

CHAPTER
THIRTEEN

"For What It's Worth" – Buffalo Springfield

Taking a cab from Stefan's apartment, they first tried to file a Missing Persons report at the main police station, but were told that they had to file it in the precinct where Miklos lived—in Brooklyn. There, they were told to wait, because there was no one to take their complaint. Finally, they wrote out a report, only to be told that they could not leave until they first spoke with the detectives upstairs. There, Detectives Tritt and Hagen interrogated them as if Maddy and Stefan were suspects in some criminal activity. "Why exactly do you think this guy is missing? He could be on a business trip; he could be having an affair." Maddy repeated to them everything that she had written in the report downstairs. Then they required her to write a second report for them, as if the first report did not exist.

She was just finishing her second report when a third detective approached her and demanded to know how she got the number for Missing Persons. "Why didn't you call 911?" By this time, Maddy had reached the end of her patience. "Why am I being treated like a criminal? All I want to do is file a report on my missing boyfriend, who could very well be the floater pulled from the Hudson River, and you are raking me over the coals. Why isn't anyone willing to help? Is this how the NYPD treats people in New York? No wonder people don't want to even bother with the police. This is outrageous." The detective glared at her, "If you don't intend to cooperate, you don't need to bother filing a report—you can go." Maddy dug in her heels. "Oh, I fully intend to cooperate, but your attitude is getting in my way." He sneered, "You're the one with the attitude problem, lady." Maddy was losing her temper, when suddenly a man walked up to her and asked, "What's happening here?"

She turned to him and asked, "Are you a detective?" "No, I'm Carl—I left a message on your answering machine in Atlanta, remember?" Somehow Carl knew what she looked like and thought Maddy would recognize him, but she had never seen him before. But before Maddy could say anything to him, Carl started talking with the detectives and suddenly they all left together, walking to a back room without saying another word to Maddy. She gave Stefan a look as if to say, "What just happened?" but Stefan just shrugged his shoulders and shook his head. When Carl and the detectives returned, they were talking among themselves about Miklos and referred to Maddy in the third person, as if she was not even in the same room. Maddy overheard them talking about "photos of the body", and she heard Carl say, "Well, I looked at them, but I can't say definitely it is him. We'll have to go to the ME's office to get them to confirm it."

Now Maddy was enraged. She had just spent the last four hours trying to get anyone in the NYPD to accept the fact that Miklos was even missing! Then, in a matter of minutes, a stranger walked in, instantly commanded the full attention of all three detectives and was apparently given a private viewing of photos of a body that might be Miklos! A private investigation had just been launched by a complete stranger—this man who introduced himself as Carl, while Maddy fought to get the detectives to even take her report! Now, Maddy had been reduced to an unnecessary bystander. Detective Tritt handed Maddy his card while saying to Carl, "Be here at 10:30. She'll need to call in the morning before showing up here." Carl said, "Don't worry about it; I'll call," and disappeared down a hallway. Maddy was seething but fought to maintain her composure. She looked at the card the detective had handed her: Miklos had been assigned a case number by the precinct.

A fourth detective walked up and said, "We need a copy of his passport—I'll take you back to the apartment to get it." Stefan and Maddy followed him to the car. When they arrived at Christophe's apartment, the detective said, "If it's okay, I'll just drop you off here—can you take a cab back to the station?" Maddy and Stefan agreed, because they didn't know any better.

When they returned to the precinct, no one was there to take the passport. They sat and waited. When Detective Tritt arrived, he asked why the detective who drove them was not with them. They explained that he had just dropped them off, so they took a cab back to the precinct. The detective made a photocopy of the passport, handed it back, and told them to return to the precinct at 10:30 a.m. the next morning, because they had to be escorted by the police to the Medical Examiner's office. It did not occur to Maddy to ask why a police escort was needed to go to a public building.

The next morning, after having breakfast with Christophe, Miklos's phone rang and Maddy answered it. It was Carl, "Look, the ME office appointment has been put off till 4 p.m." But Maddy wasn't about to trust anything that Carl said, so she immediately called the precinct and was relieved when she reached a different detective. Maddy said, "What's going on? First, I'm told to come to the precinct at 10:30 because a police escort is required to go to the Medical Examiner's Office; then, this guy Carl who isn't even with the police department calls me and says it's been put off till 4:00—but no one from the precinct tells me this directly?" The detective sounded puzzled, "Look, uh, I don't know why you were told that you have to have a police escort to go to the ME's office because it's a public office—anyone can go there any time it's open." Maddy said, "That suits me—just give me the ME's office number so I can confirm this." He gave her the address and phone number. Maddy immediately recognized the phone number as that of the morgue and was reassured. They had been very helpful and straightforward the day before. When she called, the staff member said, "Absolutely, we're here—just come any time." Maddy said, "I'm on my way."

When Maddy walked out of Miklos's room, Christophe said, "I'm not sure how he got my number, but Carl has been calling trying to reach you—he said your number was busy. I told him not to tie up the line, because I had my own matters to attend to." Maddy grinned and thanked him—Christophe was quickly becoming a trusted friend.

Stefan arrived, but had not slept all night. He was visibly shaken, pacing back and forth in front of her and was pleading with Maddy not to go to the Medical Examiner's Office. He said, "Look, I'm sure that Miklos is alive; we just have to keep looking—we can't just give up like this—it's like we're deciding that he's dead." Maddy sat him down and said, "Stefan, I loved Miklos, and believe me, I wish that he could be alive still—just as much as you do—but I believe in my heart that the body lying in the morgue is Miklos. Now, you and Christophe both called me and asked me to come here and investigate his disappearance—and I owe it to Miklos to do everything I can. I would want someone who loves me to do the same thing for me—wouldn't you? Now if you will just help me catch a cab and take me to the ME's office, you do not have to go into the building—I will take it from there—you can just keep going, okay?" Stefan sighed, and said, "All right." He seemed relieved, as though the ME's office represented death itself—and if he did not enter the building, then he would not have to face it—he could still believe it wasn't true. Meanwhile, both Christophe's and Miklos's phones were ringing off the hook. They all ignored the ringing; it had to be Carl trying to track them down.

When Maddy walked into the lobby of ME's office, Carl was there to meet her. Maddy was not surprised; she deliberately walked right past him without saying a word and approached a female detective who was there. She was reassured when the detective explained that the precinct had misled Maddy, and that there was no need for a police escort. They had been trying to call her to tell her that, but no one had answered at the phone number she had provided. Maddy said, "Well, it's been a crazy morning—sorry." The female detective was the first officer to treat Maddy with respect for the situation and for her loss. She looked Maddy in the eyes when she spoke with her. Maddy was so grateful, she wanted to hug the officer. Maddy was given a card with the Case Number that had been assigned to Miklos by the ME office. Maddy stared at the card. The man she had loved was now a body bag with a case number.

Maddy completed a form for the ME staff member, but had to leave many sections blank: Miklos's mother's maiden name; the address of his parents' apartment in Budapest; his dentist's name. She promised that she would find out the information in the next day and call with the information. She asked the staff member when an autopsy would be performed, when the body could be released for cremation, and when would a cause of death be determined. The staff member explained that everything would be on hold pending a definitive match to the dental records. Maddy promised to obtain the records.

Maddy was then taken to a small room by the ME staff member, but she was startled to see several male detectives standing in the room. She thought, "If no police escort was required—if anyone can go to the ME's office, why are they here?" But before she could say anything, one of the detectives said, "If the dental records are a match, we will need you to call the precinct and provide a detailed reason if you do not believe it is a suicide." Maddy was ready to question that, when the detective said, "There is no reason for you to view the photos of the body, so you can go." Maddy felt the blood rush to her face as she remembered being in the precinct office the night before and having to listen to Carl tell the detectives that after looking at the photos he wasn't sure it was Miklos—why was a stranger allowed to see the photos but she wasn't given the same privilege?

Taking a deep breath, Maddy tried to remain calm and said, "I appreciate that, but the only person to have seen pictures of the body is practically a stranger to me and a complete stranger to his family in Budapest. When I have to place Miklos's ashes in his mother's hands, I will have to look her in the eyes and answer the question, 'Is this really my son?' I will have to say, 'I saw the pictures, and I know this is Miklos.' And because I have slept in her apartment, because I have eaten at her table and because I have loved her son, she will believe me—she will know that I speak the truth from my heart."

One of the detectives addressed the ME staff member and said, "Okay, show her the photos." Now Maddy was seething. The detectives were not only telling the ME office how to run its business but were intruding into a very private moment. They actually expected her to undergo the ordeal of looking at photos of the decomposed body of a loved one surrounded by a roomful of detectives! She took another deep breath and said, "Clear the room now." The detective said, "No, there must be a detective present." "Fine. If that's true, you get one." Everyone left except one male detective and the ME staff member. Maddy said, "I have to pray first." They said, "Okay." Maddy closed her eyes and asked God to allow her to look at the photos, ask pertinent questions, and make or reject the identification, but not be haunted by the images afterward—not to have any specific recollection of the images after viewing them. She opened her eyes and was shown three photographs. She asked about the markings on the skull. Then she said, "These are Miklos's teeth. I've dated a lot of men, but Miklos was the only one with perfect teeth. I will get the dental records for you. But I know they will match."

One of the detectives offered to drive Maddy back to Christophe's apartment, but just as they were leaving, Carl appeared out of nowhere and said, "I'll go with you." In the car, as if to remind Maddy that he had been shown the photos first, Carl said, "You did notice, didn't you that his teeth were pushed back at an angle—I thought that was strange." Maddy was fighting to control her anger and said, "You know, I think it is interesting that you noticed that. I didn't." Maddy was thinking to herself, "You say one more word to me, Carl, just one more word, and my right hand to God, there will be a fresh body in that morgue, and I promise you, it won't be mine."

CHAPTER
FOURTEEN

"I'll Stand By You" – The Pretenders

When Maddy returned to Miklos's room, she found the number for Miklos's parents in Budapest, but no one answered. With all that had been happening, she had forgotten that when they were in Budapest Miklos told her about the cabin where the family always spends the summer months. She found the number of Miklos's dentist and left a message explaining who she was and why she needed a copy of his dental records and x-rays. She said she would be at his office at 9:00 a.m. Monday morning to pick them up. Then she called Stefan to tell him everything that had happened at the ME office. Stefan sounded tired; Maddy begged him to get some rest and eat something.

Maddy called the publishing company; the owner suggested that they meet at a restaurant that evening, so he could give her the draft of the manual and go over the revisions. She promised to be there, but said she would call the restaurant to get word to him if she were running late.

Miklos's phone rang, and it was his ex-father-in-law, Nathan. Maddy explained who she was and why she was answering Miklos's phone. She told him about the rental car and the morgue. Nathan said that the last time he saw Miklos was when he was helping him prepare his taxes. Miklos's small painting business was barely making it, and he was depressed—it was like a shadow was hanging over him that he couldn't shake. Nathan had suggested to Miklos that he get away from it all for a while and said that he was going to Toronto for a few days, why didn't Miklos come along? But Miklos had said that he had too much going on to leave. Nathan said, "I just wanted to check in on him... I thought he would be there... I guess I was too late...."

Maddy asked, "Are you thinking that if you had convinced him to go with you to Toronto that Miklos would be alive now?" Nathan sighed and said, "Actually, yes." Maddy said, "You know that we can't change people, no matter what we do—we have to accept the dark and the light in them, even if it kills them—it's always their choice, not ours. You might have delayed whatever got him killed, but you could not have prevented it." Nathan was silent. Maddy told him about carbon copy of the check for digital design classes dated the same day Miklos disappeared. She also told him about the gun license she had found and her theory that whatever got him killed was the reason for both—that he was paying for school by doing something that scared him enough to want a gun for protection.

Nathan said, "But I would have given him the money for school if he had just asked." Maddy said, "And I suggested that he form an LLC with investors to raise the money, but he was too proud. He was too proud to ask you, and he was too proud to ask other investors." Nathan was struggling, "If I just had one more chance…." Maddy said, "You couldn't have changed his pride—he wanted to find his own answers, even if those answers led him to dark places. We all have a dark side—it just doesn't get us all killed."

There was silence on the phone, and then Nathan said, "You know I honestly loved him like a son." Maddy said, "And he loved you as though you were his father—he told me how much it meant to him that you built a studio for him and believed in his success as an artist. You know he never got that from his own father growing up. You gave him your time and your love—that's everything. You made a difference in his life, but the cruel truth is that popular songs aside, love can't solve everything—it doesn't take away free will. I gave Miklos a choice eight months ago to open his heart and let me in; he chose to keep his walls up. He wanted to be on his own. I walked away—but I walked away in love and that shocked him, because he had never had anyone do that before. I wanted Miklos to work on the kind of self-love that leads to the ability to love others. Instead, he hunkered down and the walls closed in around him. I understood Miklos, because we had a lot in common: I had an abusive parent who couldn't show me love; I struggled to see myself as loveable—through school, through the old-boy networks at work and through meaningless relationships. But I started therapy and joined a church where God is a healer, teaching self-love, acceptance and bridge-building. I wanted that for Miklos but he wasn't ready."

"Where do you think God is in all this now?" Nathan asked. Maddy drew a breath, "I think that if God truly knew that Miklos was not ready to face his darkness in this lifetime, then God also knew that he would go down that dark path, be totally controlled by it and be unable to protect those around him. I take comfort in the fact that Miklos wasn't on that path for very long—maybe a matter of months, and he did not take anyone else with him when it was his time to go. The rest of us—those who loved him—were protected from the path that took his life. I believe that God wants only our highest good."

Nathan asked, "Do you believe in reincarnation?" "I do," said Maddy, "I believe that on the other side of the veil, we are in spirit and we get to look at the incarnation we just left and decide what lessons we want to learn next. Each soul is on a very different journey, so we can't compare ourselves to others—just learn what we can." Maddy then told Nathan that she did not believe that Miklos took his own life; he was renting cars because he was following instructions, "Now I don't know who was giving him those instructions or what they were telling him to do. But I do know that he realized the danger involved—that's why he wanted a gun. I believe those dangerous people killed Miklos because he was expendable: he had no family, no criminal record; his body would probably never be identified. Miklos was just a foot soldier; who knows—maybe he refused to follow the next set of instructions, so they killed him. We will never know." They talked a bit longer, and Maddy promised to let Nathan know whether the dental records matched; then they hung up.

Sitting on Miklos's bed, Maddy went over the conversation with Nathan in her head. She suddenly remembered her labyrinth walk months earlier when she asked God to show her the way ahead: was Miklos's death part of the "bigger picture" that Spirit asked her to wait to see? Was this what Spirit meant when it said that she would "soon see why everything was happening as it should"?

Maddy again tried to reach Miklos's parents at their apartment in Budapest, but there was still no answer. She found an old Hungarian-English dictionary in Miklos's desk and realized that she would probably need it to be able to speak some basic phrases if she called anyone else, because she could not assume people there would speak English. She prayed that whoever she reached would be able to help. She called his sister, Korinna, whom she had met while in Budapest. Korinna did not speak English, but eventually, translating one word at a time, Maddy understood that everyone was away at the cabin and that his sister had to stay in the city for work. Maddy did her best using the dictionary to tell her that her brother was missing and possibly dead and that Maddy needed to reach her mother. Korinna was in shock. After some time, Korinna offered to call the post office near the cabin and have someone bring Zsófia to the post office to use the phone. They agreed that noon Budapest time (6 a.m. New York time) would be a good time for his mother to call Maddy. By the end of the phone call, both Maddy and Korinna were crying.

When she hung up, she looked at the clock and realized that she was supposed to be meeting the owner of the publishing company at the restaurant. She called the restaurant and asked them to page him; when he came to the phone, Maddy explained that she was running late but she was on her way. He said, "No problem, I'm here with my wife outside on their patio—it's a fine evening, we're having drinks and I'm happy to wait." Maddy arrived at the restaurant, and they treated her to dinner as she told them the saga of the last 48 hours. As the conversation drifted into the manual and other things, the owner managed to do what no one else had done: got her to laugh and relax. Maddy could feel herself recharging and was so grateful. The publishing company owner insisted on paying for her cab ride back to Christophe's apartment, and Maddy thanked him for everything he had done.

Christophe was waiting with a pot of tea and cookies, and they sat for a long time in his living room, going over everything that had happened. He volunteered to go with Maddy to get the dental records the next morning, and she gratefully accepted his offer. As she got ready to sleep a second night in Miklos's bed, she realized that she was surrounded by angels in human form, and in her head was playing Toni Childs, "Walk and Talk Like Angels"—now it was time for Maddy to put aside her fears.

CHAPTER
FIFTEEN

"You Can Do This Hard Thing" – Carrie Newcomer

Monday morning at 5:30 a.m., the phone rang. It was Zsófia phoning from the post office outside Budapest. In her fear and confusion, she had lost her understanding of a second language—she was speaking only in Hungarian. Maddy grabbed the dictionary, so she could follow what Zsófia was saying. Eventually, she understood. Zsófia asked, "Where is my son? Is he there? Why are you in New York? Why can't I speak with my son?" Maddy's hands shook as she grabbed the phrases she had written out in Hungarian and then used the dictionary to try to explain more. She told Zsófia that Miklos had been missing for 20 days, that a rental car had been found, that the morgue had a body, that Maddy had seen photos of the body but it was too bad to recognize but the teeth looked like those of Miklos—and the body had his build. She told Zsófia that tomorrow the dental records would determine the identity. They were both crying; Maddy told Zsófia that she knew that Miklos loved her more than anything.

Zsófia said that the post office was closing, and Maddy could hear men's voices in the background yelling. Zsófia was slowly recovering her ability to speak English and said, "When will you know?" Maddy said, "Tomorrow. The body is very bad. Do you believe in cremation? Do you cremate bodies in Hungary?" Zsófia said, "Yes. Would it be done in New York?" Maddy said, "Yes. It would be too expensive to ship the body—and if it will be cremated anyway, it can be cremated here." Zsófia asked Maddy to please handle everything, and Maddy promised that she would. They agreed that Zsófia would call the same time the next day, and hung up after both saying, "I love you, thank you." Maddy collapsed on the floor of Miklos's room, sobbing so hard that she was shaking. When she finally was able to walk out to go to the kitchen to get some water, Christophe was there. He put his arms around Maddy and said, "This is the hardest thing you will ever have to do in your entire life. Nothing else your whole life will ever be this hard." Maddy said, "Oh, Christophe, I pray you are right, because I don't think I can do anything more difficult than this."

At 8:30 a.m. the next morning, Christophe and Maddy left for the office of Miklos's dentist. They had the telephone number from Miklos's address book, but had not been able to find the address in the phone directory. So Christophe had to do some investigating to find it. They arrived at the office at 9:15, and the dentist met them in the waiting room. He was a kind and gentle man. He said that he had retrieved Maddy's message yesterday and had written out a chart for the ME's office. He said, "I am very sorry you are going through this." Maddy burst into tears. Her hands shook holding the large envelope, realizing that it held the key to Miklos's disappearance: his only remaining means of identification. Fortunately, there was a small wooded park just outside the dentist's office, and Christophe sat there with Maddy on a bench until she had recovered. Christophe helped Maddy get a cab and let her out at the ME's office. He said, "You have my number. Call if you need anything."

Inside the ME's office, the staff member who greeted Maddy was the same one whom she had met the day before, and she handed her the dental records. Maddy was given the name and phone number of the physician who would be confirming the dental records match; she said the results should be back by 3:00 p.m. The staff member also said that the autopsy had actually been performed the day after the body was pulled from the water, so the results could be given to Maddy as soon as the dental records match was confirmed. She said that if Maddy didn't want to wait until 3, she could leave a message with a callback number on the physician's answering machine—that way the physician could call Maddy earlier if the results were known. The staff member also told Maddy to go ahead and contact a funeral home; that way when the match is known, Maddy could make arrangements and the body could be moved. Maddy thanked the staff member for being so clear and helpful, "Whatever you are being paid, it is not nearly enough for the job that you are doing—really. You are a blessing in the middle of a nightmare. Please know how much I appreciate your help."

Maddy left and went to a market in the next block; she bought lunch and some groceries to keep in Christophe's refrigerator. As she got on the bus to return to Christophe's apartment, she realized that she felt as though she was in silent slow motion while the world around her was noisily moving at laser speed. She knew she was in shock.

Back in Miklos's room, Maddy called the physician's number that had been given to her by the ME staff member. Without listening to the recording on the physician's answering machine, Maddy hurriedly left a message and gave Miklos's phone number. Her message never recorded, because she failed to press the pound sign twice as the recording instructed.

Suddenly, she remembered that her return flight to Atlanta was leaving in an hour. Maddy called and rescheduled the flight for Wednesday morning, hoping that this ordeal would be over by then. Next, she called the first funeral home on the list that the ME office had given her. The director advised Maddy to have a fax sent from Hungary signed by a family member (mother, sister, etc.) authorizing cremation. He dictated the words for the fax. He explained that as soon as Maddy signed the contract for cremation and submitted payment the body would be retrieved from the morgue. Once the fax was received, the body would be cremated. The ashes could be sent to Maddy back in Atlanta by U.S. mail. Maddy promised the director that she would call him to set up a meeting once she had worked everything out with the family.

Maddy ate the lunch she bought in the market while she told Christophe everything she had learned, and then she returned to Miklos's room to take a nap. When she woke up, it was 2:00 p.m., and she left another message for the physician, but she still didn't listen to the recorded instructions. After 30 minutes, Maddy called again and this time listened to the instructions, realized her mistake, pushed the pound sign twice and recorded her message. At 3:15, the physician called and confirmed: the records were a perfect match; the coroner would call her with the autopsy results later. Maddy said, "Thank you for confirming what I already knew in my heart."

Then Maddy called Stefan and told him the dental records were a perfect match, that she had talked to Miklos's mother who had asked her to handle the arrangements with the funeral home. But she was caught off-guard when Stefan exploded in anger, "You had no right to make those decisions. You shouldn't be doing any of this!" Maddy, took a deep breath and said, "Stefan, I was on the phone with his sister Korinna for a long time yesterday and with his mother Zsófia this morning; believe me when I tell you that I am not making any decisions—his mother is the sole decision maker, and I will honor her wishes. Nothing will be final until the fax is received from Hungary with the signature of a family member. I am not legally allowed to make any decisions—I am not a family member." Stefan muttered, "Well, all right," and hung up abruptly. Even though Maddy understood in her head that it was Stefan's grief showing itself as anger, her heart still hurt, and it took a while for Maddy to recover.

Next Maddy called Miklos's ex-father-in-law as she had promised to do. Nathan offered to pay for the cremation, and Maddy gratefully accepted his kind generosity. He said, "I have to ask, though, why are the ashes going to you in Atlanta instead of to Budapest?" Maddy said, "Nathan, I find it surreal that I am going to walk into a Post Office in Atlanta and some well-intentioned postal employee is going to simply hand me Miklos in a box. I could never put Zsófia through that. I will fly to Budapest with his ashes, place them in her hands and hold her as she sobs." Nathan stammered, "Oh, uh, yes. I understand completely now. I'm sorry—that makes total sense." Nathan also offered to handle the storage of Miklos's belongings until Maddy could come back to New York and sort through them.

The last call was to the precinct to report the dental records match and advise them that the case number could now be attached to Miklos Takács. Maddy was told to come back to the precinct to fill out yet another report to explain why she did not believe it was a suicide. Maddy agreed and also provided them with her contact information back in Atlanta.

She sat on Miklos's bed, staring at all the papers, visualizing them as puzzle pieces that she was trying to put together to solve the mystery of his disappearance. She was hearing Guns n' Roses in her head singing "Knockin' on Heaven's Door." That "long black cloud" felt heavy around Maddy now.

CHAPTER SIXTEEN

"If I Have to Go" – Tom Waits

After the dinner that Christophe had prepared for them both, Maddy decided to go through Miklos's bookcase. It was full of art books, but then she spotted a small book on the Mafia—the Italian organized crime syndicate. She suddenly remembered a phone conversation when they were first dating when Miklos told her that he had been out at a club and caught a glimpse of John Gotti, Jr., a member of that syndicate—and Maddy was alarmed that Miklos sounded absolutely giddy, as if he had seen a movie star! Then she remembered another conversation when they were in Hungary in which he told her about coming to America. He said that when he had out-stayed his visa, he met members of an organized crime syndicate who hid him and arranged for him to work at an art gallery that could pay him under the table. Maddy recalled being frightened when Miklos told her that story, "Why on earth would you look for such people—and why would you trust them?" Miklos had replied, "Rózsa, growing up in Budapest the black market—the crime organization—was how families got meat on the table—everyone knew people in criminal organizations, because under Communism, they ran the marketplace." Maddy got a cold chill when she remembered her response to him, "Well, sugar, in the U.S. organized crime is how people get killed."

Suddenly, a lightbulb clicked on in Maddy's head: Miklos must have sought out those same men—the men who had helped him a decade earlier: Miklos must have told them that he needed to make some quick cash. So they gave him driving jobs to do. The puzzle pieces finally snapped together in Maddy's mind. "That is why I was haunted by the song 'Gangsta's Paradise' for weeks before I even knew Miklos was missing!" I was being given a sign from guides on the other side of the veil to help prepare me for what I was about to learn: the money and power, the guns and the danger—and the choir."

Maddy went back to the gun license receipt and the photocopy of the list of gun laws. Turning the photocopy over, she saw something she had missed earlier: hand written notes by Miklos that said, "red Ford Explorer" and the address of the rental car company that Maddy had called her first day there. Maddy was stunned. Someone had dictated to him what color and model of vehicle to rent (perhaps so they could recognize that it was him when he arrived) and where to go to rent the vehicle. She thought, "Well, it's no accident that he wrote the instructions on the back of the gun information—whatever he was being instructed to do was the reason he needed a gun in the first place." Was Miklos delivering contraband and receiving large amounts of cash? Maybe the first driving job he did back in July was easy, so he agreed to do a second job for a longer period of time. Maybe he thought he could juggle his workload by driving at night and completing his painting jobs in the daytime. But something went terribly wrong on August 5th. Something that got him killed and then dumped in the Hudson River.

Now her head was spinning. Miklos hid his dark plans, his secret alliance from everyone. He hid the rental car, the gun license—everything. But he couldn't hide his own disappearance—not even in a body bag. Maybe he thought it would work out this time just as it had in the '80's: a green card, a private painting studio and an amazing father-in-law. Maybe he had a vision of recreating that Camelot-like existence—escaping the drudgery of meaningless faux finishing jobs to learn digital art and digital animation—dreaming of jobs with DreamWorks or Pixar. But this time, the underworld was looking for an obedient and expendable foot soldier with no family, no criminal record and no fingerprints on file—someone who would be disposable if he proved to be disobedient. "Oh, babe, you thought you could use them, but they were using you—and when they were finished, so were you," Maddy sighed. She went to sleep with the Rolling Stones "Slipping Away" playing in her head: all you wanted was ecstasy, Miklos, but you didn't get much.

CHAPTER
SEVENTEEN

"Prayer for the Dying" – Seal

At 6:30 a.m. Tuesday, Zsófia phoned from the post office in Hungary. "Is it true: is my son dead?" "*Igen.* Yes," Maddy sobbed. Zsófia explained that she was on medication and could not travel to America. Maddy said, "Oh, of course, but we must handle the body now." She tried to get Zsófia to understand that the funeral home required a fax from a family member to authorize the cremation. Nothing could be done until the fax was received. But Zsófia was losing her capacity for a second language again. Maddy grabbed the dictionary and struggled to find the words for funeral home, cremation, fax machine and authorization. Finally, Zsófia said in English, "Yes, Korinna has a fax machine in her office in Budapest; she can send the fax from there." Zsófia begged Maddy to write a long letter as soon as she could. "I understand and I do not understand. Why did this happen? How did this happen?" Maddy promised that she would write everything she knew as soon as she could. They were both sobbing and told each other "I love you," before hanging up.

Maddy collapsed in a heap on the floor of Miklos's room. This is how sudden death feels to those left behind. Maddy had no experience with sudden death, She had lost over a dozen friends and family members throughout the years, first in grade school, then in college and continuing through the AIDS pandemic—friends and relatives lost to breast, brain, ovarian and cervical cancer, old age and AIDS—but all were slow death. There was time to adjust to the reality of it. It was not less painful, but when it happened, it did not feel strange. It was part of a larger process that had been at work—a process you hated with every fiber in your being, but one that could be grasped. No one in Miklos's life was permitted to be part of his process. He stepped into Dante's Inferno, and the river of blood ran and no one would ever know how or why.

At 7:30 a.m. Miklos's phone rang; it was Korinna and she had no idea what was going on. Maddy grabbed the Hungarian dictionary and started from the beginning again. Eventually Maddy dictated word-for-word the fax content using the dictionary. Afterward, Maddy began to box up Miklos's possessions, taking some items back to Atlanta to ship to his parents but leaving the majority of his belongings to be placed in storage in New York, since Nathan had agreed to make those arrangements. She would return to New York to sort through them after she delivered the ashes to Zsófia.

Stefan phoned and apologized for their misunderstanding. Maddy said, "You and I have been under so much stress—and a different kind of stress—one that neither of us had ever experienced before. God willing, you and I will never go through anything like this again. We should be gentle with ourselves and with each other—give ourselves permission to rage at the situation when we need to. We are human. There is nothing to forgive. We are here for each other—that is all that matters." She gave Stefan her list of meetings for the day, starting with the funeral home director, then the publishing company owner and finally the detectives. Stefan said, "You have my number—call me if you need me to do anything." She promised she would.

After the lunch that Christophe had prepared for them, Maddy spent two hours struggling to focus on the revisions to the manual that she had promised to finalize before her meeting with the owner. The phone rang: it was the coroner with the results of the autopsy: "Inconclusive." The toxicology report would not be issued for another 6-8 weeks because of the absorption of the water. The cause of death would be listed as "Undetermined." Maddy suddenly realized that she had never asked about the clothes that Miklos had been wearing when he was put in the water. The physician said, "A white t-shirt, white briefs, tan shorts, and white socks." A perfect match for the description that Jakob had given her when she asked him what he was wearing on August 5th at his loft. Maddy suddenly remembered that Miklos never went anywhere without his black leather fanny pack. But the physician said, "There was no fanny pack." Maddy had no other questions and thanked the physician for her time. After she hung up, Maddy thought about the fanny pack. It was not in the backpack or in the car; if someone had stolen it as a robbery, they would have used the credit cards that were in the billfold he kept in it. Whoever killed Miklos must have taken the fanny pack and destroyed it, not wanting to leave a trail of transactions from the credit cards.

Maddy left for the publishing company and sat in the bus in a fog. She managed to regain her focus for the meeting, and after all the revisions were discussed and finalized, she told the owner that the manual needed to be ready for her meeting in Colorado with the client in two weeks. He said that would be no problem.

The funeral home director had agreed to meet Maddy at a restaurant that was just down the street from the publishing company office. He was late and apologized profusely. Maddy shook her head and said, "This is the first time since Friday that I have been able to sit and do nothing—believe me, it was a gift." But as he handed her a pen with the contract for cremation for her signature, the pain of the last three days hit Maddy like a brick, and she burst out crying unexpectedly. There was something unbearably final about signing a document so Miklos's body could be cremated. When Maddy regained her composure, it was her turn to apologize to the director. He was gracious and understanding. Maddy knew that it came with the territory and was part of his job, but she could feel genuine compassion—and for that, she was deeply grateful.

Maddy took the bus back to Christophe's apartment and collapsed on Miklos's bed. She woke up when Christophe knocked on the door asking if she was hungry—he had made a light dinner. They ate and she told him everything that had happened that day. There was a knock at the front door, and it was Detective Morgan, who explained that he just wanted to go over everything before Maddy returned to Atlanta. Maddy showed the detective the rental car receipts, the gun license receipt, the handwritten notes, and the carbon copy of the check for digital art classes that she had found. Detective Morgan kept pressing Maddy to say it was a suicide. She pushed down her anger and said, "Why would someone who is about to commit suicide write a check for art classes? Why would he book painting jobs for the next two weeks? I refuse to believe that Miklos took his own life. He was killed somewhere and his body was dumped in that river. That is why the body was so badly decomposed. He did not jump." Detective Morgan asked about the lunch bag that Maddy had found in the rental car, so she dug it out of the trash. The receipt showed the date August 5th at 2:36 p.m. Maddy said, "So Miklos left Jakob's loft after finishing his painting samples, ate lunch and drove to meet the people who killed him." Detective Morgan said, "I'll be in touch," and left.

Maddy shook her head as she gathered up all the papers and got ready for bed. "They just want to wrap up the case with a bow and dump it in a circular file with the label 'Suicide.' Well, it's not that easy. Not for me." As she laid down, she heard a song in her head she hadn't thought of in ages: "Don't Cry My Lady Love" by Quicksilver Messenger Service. She didn't want these memories to haunt her, but she knew that they would.

CHAPTER EIGHTEEN

"Too Many Rainy Days" – The Rossington Band

At 6:30 a.m. Wednesday, Maddy woke up, packed and prepared never to see Miklos's room again. Christophe had prepared sausage and eggs, croissants, cheeses and fruit for breakfast, and Maddy found herself devouring it all as though she had not eaten in ages. Perhaps her body was finally ready to let go of all the tension that had gripped her since she arrived. She tried to tell Christophe how very much he had meant to her—how she could not have survived the last three days without him. He was humble and said, "I just did what anyone would have done." But she shook her head because she knew better. He was an angel in human form.

Rain had just started to fall as the cabbie loaded her bags and they drove to Newark. Maddy was thinking about the times that she had taken that same trip with Miklos—it was hard to wrap her mind around the fact that she would never see him again. Now the rain was pouring down in sheets, and when she checked in for her flight, she was told all flights had been cancelled. She settled into the lounge to wait and watch the rain. Maddy was wishing she could just be swallowed up by the storm.

Finally back in Atlanta, Maddy was at Sam's house, sitting in her office staring at stacks of paperwork when the phone rang. It was Detective Morgan. He said, "I need you to send me copies of all the documents you showed me. There has been a new development. It turns out that the silver Ford Escort was not towed from the George Washington Bridge—it was towed from a Port Authority employee parking lot." Maddy asked, "When was it towed?" Detective Morgan said, "August 16th." "But that was a week after they pulled the body out of the water," Maddy said. "Yes. So, you'll send me what you have?" "I will," Maddy said.

She hung up the phone with a sigh of relief and thought, "Finally, someone is telling me something that makes sense—Miklos was never on the bridge at all! He was not in the water until after he was killed, and the murderers hid the car in the parking lot. And the coroner was right: the body was too badly decomposed to have been in water for four days straight—it probably was dumped in the water the same day it was found—so the decomposition happened because the body was out of the water for four days." As horrifying as all this was to consider, it was a great relief to Maddy. It confirmed her belief that Miklos's death was not a suicide. It was a vindication of what she had believed in her heart the entire time.

Suddenly, Maddy remembered what the man at the rental car company had said on August 24th, "It's being towed into our garage right now." But the car was actually towed eight days earlier, and it had never been on the bridge at all—so he lied about everything. Why? And how was it all connected? There were so many leftover puzzle pieces. She immediately called Stefan and told him the news. Then she drove to a nearby copy center to drop off all the documents to be photocopied.

Two weeks later, Maddy was in Colorado for her meeting with her client. She had just checked into the hotel, had verified that the manuals arrived as scheduled and was unpacking when the phone in her hotel room rang. The caller identified himself as a detective with the NYPD, but Maddy had never heard his name or his voice before. She asked, "Is there news about Miklos's case?" He said in a slow and hushed tone, "No, I just wanted you to know… that I could find you." A cold chill ran down Maddy's spine as she slammed the receiver down on the phone cradle; she sat down on the bed, shaking. But once she recovered, she was puzzled: it didn't make any sense that the caller was from the NYPD, because her last contact was with Detective Morgan, who was so helpful and supportive—he was trying to get to the bottom of what really happened. Someone was definitely trying to frighten her—who was it really? And why was he trying to scare her? What did they think she was going to do? How was she a threat to them?

CHAPTER
SIXTEEN

"Many a Mile to Freedom" – Traffic

When Maddy saw the pink "sorry we missed you" registered mail notice, she knew that the parcel was from the funeral home. The drive to the Post Office seemed to take forever, and when she got to the counter, the postal worker took her notice and cheerfully said, "Oh, something from Victoria's Secret?" Maddy burst out crying—it came from nowhere. The postal worker was startled, immediately apologized and practically ran to get the package. Maddy was still standing at the counter crying when she heard, "Maddy, is that you?" She turned and realized it was Stan—someone with whom she had a very complicated relationship years earlier. Wiping her face, she said, "Uh, yes, hi Stan." He said, "What's wrong? How can I help?" The postal worker was back at the counter now and awkwardly said, "Uh, excuse me, ma'am, please, your package? I just need your signature." She signed the receipt and then stared blankly at the package." Stan was up at the counter now, taking her arm and saying, "Let's just walk over here, okay?" Maddy muttered something unintelligible as her eyes were still transfixed on the package in her arms, and they walked out of the post office.

Stan said, "Maddy, talk to me, what's going on? Are you sick? Do you need to go to the hospital?" She took a deep breath and said, "The man I was dating was murdered and these are his ashes." "Oh my God. Okay, uh, let's walk to your car, and I can follow you home, how does that sound?" Are you still living at the same place?" He still had her arm, and she felt as though she was in a trance—she heard herself said, "Yes, please, that would be good. Um. Actually I've moved." And she gave him Sam's address so he would know where she was going.

She didn't remember the drive home, but when Maddy unlocked the front door, Stan followed her in. She had just put the package down on the coffee table when she turned around to find Stan right behind her. He put his arms around her and pulled her close to him. Suddenly,

Maddy snapped back to reality and pulled away. She looked at Stan as if she was suddenly seeing him for the first time and said, "Stan, grief makes people do really stupid things, and I don't want you to be one of the stupid things that I do out of grief. Now, I appreciate you making sure I got home okay, but I think you really need to leave now." Stan stuttered, "Uh, oh, well, um, sure, I get it. I'm gone." Maddy locked the door behind him and sat down. She stared at the package and thought, "My God, this is what is left of you Miklos." She flashed back to the Post Office and how it felt signing for the package. She thought, "Oh, thank God I didn't put your mother through this—it would have killed her. Hell, it nearly killed me." Then she thought of Stan and shook her head—God certainly chose an unusual angel to help her this time!

In the months that followed, Maddy's life was hectic. After long talks with the rector of her Episcopal Church and with the seminary admission officials, Maddy decided to apply for a dual degree master's program at the same seminary the rector had attended. It would require taking the Graduate Record Examination and taking a foreign language class. Zsófia had asked her to administer Miklos's estate in New York, so there was a lot of paperwork involved: accounts to close and creditors to notify. Also, Miklos's belongings were still in storage and had to be sorted. Maddy was still working as a consultant, but had notified her clients that she was moving to attend graduate school in the coming year. She arranged for her flight to Budapest to leave mid-December, right after she sat for the GRE.

This time packing for Budapest, Maddy knew to prepare for the weather and the dry heat of the apartment. She remembered packing for the trip just 12 months earlier—how excited she had been packing the presents she had bought, how anxious she had been to finish the quilt and how nervous she had been not knowing what to expect in Budapest. Now she was a jumble of emotions. She felt a sense of relief that Miklos's spirit could finally be at peace: his parents could find closure, and what remained of his body would be home at last. She longed to see Zsófia and be with someone who shared her grief. Yet, she was a bit confused when she thought about how strange it would feel to return to Atlanta afterward, with the ordeal finally behind her.

Maddy had felt so alone in her grief—her friends and her priest were wonderfully supportive, of course, but the circumstances did not fit into any category: she had not lost a husband; she had not lost someone she was even dating at the time of his death; instead, she had lost a former boyfriend. How do you explain that to anyone? How do you explain to someone that grief is still grief, regardless of the complexity of the situation?

On the trip to Budapest, Maddy carried Miklos's ashes with her in her backpack through each international customs line and placed him on the conveyor belt to be x-rayed at every terminal. She stoically answered the "What is in this box?" question asked by each well-meaning agent, and watched as each was left speechless and embarrassed by her answer. When she landed in Budapest and saw Zsófia waiting for her, the tears welled up immediately. They stood sobbing and holding each other in the airport for a long time before Maddy slipped off her backpack, took out the package and handed it to Zsófia. They walked arm-in-arm out of the airport.

"Come, I show you the place," Emil said in English, as they walked into the cemetery where Miklos's ashes had just been interred. Zsófia explained how Miklos was related to everyone else on the headstone whose ashes were also interred there. The date that Miklos's body was pulled from the water was used as a date of death on the headstone, just as it was on the death certificate. It was bitter cold, but Maddy sat on the ground staring at the headstone for a long time. Turning, she could see the statue of an angel on another headstone just across from his—appearing to reach her arms out to Miklos to protect his resting place. Maddy finally got up and walked arm-in-arm with Zsófia out of the cemetery.

On the flight back to Atlanta from Budapest, Maddy was hearing Madonna in her head singing "I'll Remember You." "Yes," Maddy thought, "Miklos, you gave me so much strength—I just didn't know how much I would need it. And yes, I definitely have a reason to cry now."

CHAPTER SEVENTEEN

"I Hear My Train A-Comin'" – Jimi Hendrix

Settling into her seat on the return New York to Atlanta Amtrak run, Maddy was glad that the train car wasn't very full. She didn't feel like having to make "polite conversation" with a stranger. It had been a difficult extended weekend. Traveling to New York this time, she knew exactly what she would be facing: the requisite meeting with the bank on Friday to close Miklos's accounts as the Administratrix of his estate and clearing out the storage unit full of painting supplies, clothes, furniture and paperwork on Saturday.

This trip she had not been able to stay with Christophe: the room that had belonged to Miklos was now rented to someone else. Life goes on. So a friend of Stefan took her in. She had not really talked much with Stefan since last summer, so there was a lot to tell him when they met on Friday afternoon. She told him that the toxicology report came back negative except for a trace of alcohol; she described her trip to deliver the ashes to Miklos's parents. Then she told him about the phone call she had received in her hotel room in Colorado that had frightened her. Stefan was shocked. "But Maddy, who was it?" "I don't know—I never heard from him again. I can only tell you what I feel in my gut: that it was someone in the organized crime syndicate that employed Miklos as a driver. Maybe he knew Carl—maybe he had friends in the precinct—maybe he had powerful friends who could track my whereabouts—who knows?" Now a wave of fear was crossing Stefan's face, "But Maddy, they could be watching you now—they could be watching both of us! If they could kill Miklos, they could kill us too!" Stefan appeared visibly shaken.

It was true that Maddy had felt as though there were "eyes" on her the entire time she was in New York this trip. She had purchased her first cell phone before leaving, and one of her girlfriends kept calling her on it, begging Maddy to leave New York, convinced that Maddy was in mortal danger. Maddy told Stefan the same thing she told her girlfriend, "You know that if they wanted me gone, I would already be dead. They could get that job done anywhere, any time. That man told me he could find me anywhere I went, and I believe him. But really, I think they are just watching to see what my next move will be— to see whether I will make trouble for them. Maybe they know now that I am not here to cause any trouble for anyone—I am just here to settle the last of Miklos's affairs, and they could not care less about that." Stefan was not convinced and said, "Maybe we should let Nathan take care of what's in the storage unit; maybe it would be best to leave well enough alone; maybe you should just go back to Atlanta."

Maddy looked a long time at Stefan and said, "I know none of this makes any sense to anyone else; but I know Zsófia and just having the 35 mm slides of Miklos's artwork that I sent her is not enough. She wants to hold his clothes—smell them—envision how he looked in them, see his notebooks full of sketches, listen to his music tapes—feel connected to him. No parent should lose a child—they aren't supposed to go first. If a few possessions help her find closure, then it is the least I can do to pack them up and send them to her. But Stefan, I promise, if anything happens to frighten me—to make me fear for my safety or yours, I will leave."

She asked Stefan if he had been able to find out any more information about Carl, but Stefan said that he had never seen him before that night in the precinct—and had not seen him since. As far as Stefan knew, Carl had not made any attempt to contact him, and he was relieved about that. Maddy was grateful that Miklos had sheltered all of his friends—including Maddy—from the dark side of his life, never allowing them to interact with any members of organized crime.

Stefan had been in touch with Jakob, who had agreed to take Miklos's art supplies and painting tools. Nathan had arranged for Goodwill to come to the storage unit and take everything that was left after Maddy went through it. Maddy asked Stefan if there was anything he wanted, but he said that the memories of the good times he shared with Miklos were all he needed. Maddy shuddered as she loaded clothing, notebooks, cassette tapes and papers into the expandable rolling duffel bag that Miklos had taken to Budapest on the Christmas visit they had taken together. Back then it had been filled with presents and warm clothes. It felt strange to realize that once she arrived back in Atlanta and shipped the bag off to Zsófia, the odyssey of Miklos's death would really be over. She hoped she would never have to come back to New York— or if she did, that these wounds would be healed by then.

Maddy stared out of the train car window, while the train lumbered toward Atlanta, and she remembered her first train ride, taken with her mother when she was in grade school. Her mother was job-hunting and had planned a trip over the Christmas holiday that circled the entire United States to visit relatives and interview at various universities. Maddy had fallen in love with the gentle rocking motion of the train; she was mesmerized watching the landscape slowly change from rolling hills to plains to mountains to shore to desert and back again. On that trip so long ago, it had been colder emotionally in the train car with her mother than the outside temperature, but this trip was the opposite—so full of love. Now Maddy's head was filled with the Doobie Brothers singing "Long Train Runnin' "—oh Miklos, where would you be now— without love?

EPILOGUE

"There's a Thorntree in My Garden" – Derek and the Dominos

After returning to Atlanta, Maddy saw a notice at an art store about an open call for artists, poets and performance artists to submit works to be included in a community exhibit at a local gallery. Acceptance into the exhibit was not based on formal art standards, but rather on a clear expression of a heartfelt concern or vision. Maddy found a piece of black linen and embroidered a single white rose in a clear vase—remembering that Miklos had always called her Rózsa. For the exhibit, she

had it framed and matted side-by-side with this poem that
she wrote to accompany it:

Against the black

Of the water in which you were found

Of the decomposed body I identified

Of the NYPD detective's slicked-back
hair

Of the clothes I wore to bury you

Of the hole in your mother's heart

Of the hole in the ground in Budapest

that holds your ashes

Rises the white rose

A symbol of new beginning

Opening to new possibilities

Soft and fragile, yet stronger for the
darkness

Iridescent, shining with faith deepened
by loss

Sweet with the fragrance of hope

From a clear vase

Never again to cling to walls

Never again to bury fears, dreams or soul

There is too little time for that.

About the Author

Lilli Lindbeck resides in Atlanta, Georgia, where she enjoys a wide range of activities, both spiritual and creative. She surrounds herself with music, dance and art and considers herself to be a "hopeful" romantic.

Acknowledgement

This book is dedicated to Jason, who believed in it and supported it. The author acknowledges all the angels—those still in human form and those on the other side of the veil now—who have been and remain a constant source of strength and guidance in her life. The author also owes a heartfelt debt of gratitude to her therapists, who through the years have taught her the slow process of anamnesis: remembering a trauma so that it transforms you

Thanks for reading! Please add a short review on Amazon and let me know what you thought!

Made in the USA
Monee, IL
01 March 2022

92087553R00080